Presented to:

____

By:

____

On:

____

Books by Greg Luti

Collected Poems

Everything Must Go

Day in The Life

Day in the Life

Greg Luti

gregluti.com

Edited by Greg Luti

Cover Design by Greg Luti

Cover Art by Greg Luti

Preface

I wrote this book while in college, which is why the entire thing seems so autobiographical as many of the encounters stem from real-world interactions. I was trying to be a comedian at that time too, which is where that bit of the character comes from.

I am not sure if the reader is supposed to like this main character or not, as there was a point where I remember distinctly thinking that this kid is no longer me. He is his own person, and does things that I would not do. I thought it was fitting to lean more on the punk side of his personality rather than anything else. Although I can admit that the kid is more of a punk than I ever was.

As I wrote this I didn't view him as good or bad, but just as a character that is, if that makes sense.

I wrote this originally under a pen name, but then decided years later that if I was to share it with the world, the least I can do is not hide from it.

I don't know if there is much of a plot here or even a point to this book. You can say that gives this a certain charm, I suppose.

Whenever I think about what this book is about, I always come back to the same line, it is a day in the life of this kid. He tells you about his day, what you make of it, is up to you.

I do recognize that this so-called day is not a realistic day in the fashion that I present it. This day is way too long for your average person. No one in their right mind would have this much scheduled in one day. As someone who did most of what I wrote here, I can tell you that I never came close to ever doing all of what the main character sets out to do. Most days would end when the kid leaves to go home from school. I do recognize that.

I am not sure what the reader is supposed to get out of the book, if I am honest. The kid says a lot, probably too much, and never really does anything. After reading this book, the kid stays with you afterwards, whether you like him or not.

I just remember walking around my college campus, not doing much on most days, and thinking, "What if I put all of the small moments into one book? What would that even look like?"

This book is a result of that experiment.

Greg Luti – Monday – 7/29/24

Dedication

I dedicate this book to all those classes that I never passed and to all the teachers and student who made me feel so uncomfortable in the classroom, forcing me to leave school to pursue a career as a writer on my own terms. Without you, this book would not be.

I also dedicate this to any student who ever sat in a college class and wondered what the hell they were doing there. If the school system ever failed you, and you were not sure if you were to blame or not, then this book is for you.

Table of Contents

Day in the Life

Part 1 – Introduction

Every story has a beginning, middle, and end. Or so I've been told. As I tell you this, I'll try my best to include all three components, but being the inexperienced writer that I am, I may forget some important parts that teachers preach students never to forget. Like the climax. I can't stand that I have to be told after the fact that it was the focal point of the story. Do teachers think I don't realize it's important when a main character dies in a story? I skim most of the time when I read, but I still get the idea.

I skimmed somewhere that sarcasm is hard to understand in written form, so I suggest buying the audio of this so that you can catch it when it pops up. That or I can tell you when I'm being sarcastic, but that defeats the purpose of it. It's like laughing at your own joke. I hate when people on any social network leave an unfunny joke and then put "lol" at the end of it. Okay I may not hate it, hate's a little much, but it's still a pathetic way of appreciating your unfunniness. Welcome to the Information Age, where we tell jokes one letter at a time.

Whether or not you can pick up sarcasm, you'll probably imagine my voice being different than what I actually sound like. People do that all the time. They hear themselves recorded and deny it's them. Because the recording device is just trying to play tricks on them. That's all. I got fooled once too. I can't remember when it happened but it took me some time after hearing it to realize that I sound the way I do. So when you're reading this, just remember I don't actually sound that way. That goes also if you are listening to an audio. Yeah, that guy talking is an actor. Not me.

Narrators ruin stories with all their bullshit and words. After awhile books become boring to me. I read a whole page of words just to turn the page and find there are more words to read. The whole process gets kind of repetitive, until the narrator ends it, that is. After you go through the climax and then they come to a great revelation. Like the guy was lying the whole time. The whole thing is a dream and he is dead. Narrators are stupid. Why do readers like them? I don't. I want to just slap unreliable narrators in the face. *"Hey buddy! Do you mind telling me the truth? Not that it matters. I'd just like to know when I'm talking to a liar."* I think I am a pretty reliable narrator. I never lie. Then again, I may have lied there. Whatever happens, I can't forget the climatic part of a story. And yes, I am aware of the irony behind the statement I just made. I am writing a novel complaining of its style.

Whenever I read, which isn't very much, I read enough to know literature, but not enough to say I am a real writer. By a real writer, I mean one who is actually good with words that can tell an interesting, compelling story. You may notice that my vocabulary is pretty bad. I blame that on video games and school. When I was younger, I never actually studied the vocabulary words for the tests. I just memorized how many there were of each part of speech and I'd guess from there. I'd even write on my test sheet the amount of each noun, verb, and adjective. Those were the most common. My teacher called this cheating. I didn't. I just thought it was easier than actually studying. I viewed it more as clever test taking.

See to me, the alphabet ends at the letter t. The other letters are there just so we can feel like we know more words than we really do. U – it's a vowel, so it has to be included. Other than that, no one would care much for it. V – someone looked at W and thought, "That is way too big." W – if it weren't for questions, we wouldn't want it. And then the last three letters: X, Y, and Z. Why the hell do we even have them? There are about four words we use that start with those letters. Now you see why I cheated on the test instead of learning the words. Vocabulary was never really my thing.

Anyway, there are always two things I do before I even begin sitting down with the book—I don't stand as I read and I never will. Whenever I stand with a book open, I'm probably mocking it.

First, I look for pictures. I don't care what type, what color, what size; I just want to know if they are there. If I find some, I check to see if they have captions. Good captions can make a book for me.

Second, I see how many pages there are between each chapter. It helps me to know the first chapter has six pages instead of twenty-three. Yes, I have put down books because the first chapter was thirty pages long. That book may have been the best book ever, but I gave it no chance because of that first chapter. Plus, there were no pictures in the book.

No matter what I'm reading, I always double- check those two things. I'll save you the time in case your reading habits are like mine. There are no pictures or captions in this book. There isn't even a first letter written fancy, which if I was smarter I'd know the name. Sorry to say, if I am going to get any credit as a novelist in the writing field, I can't include pictures here. My books must include words, only words. Also I'm an awful artist and I wouldn't want to pay someone to put pictures here, even if I had the money.

I would tell you the number of chapters and pages in between each chapter for this book, but I don't know that yet being I haven't finished the first chapter (obviously).

Maybe I can write like Hemingway and tell this story in five sentences. Oh, but don't worry about the short dialogue and little description I give, since the real story is from the words I don't write. Can you believe that is why that guy is praised, for stuff he didn't even write? Too bad I can't get that treatment. *"Oh he's so great. You should notice the stuff he doesn't say. They're the best."* To hell with me writing like Hemingway. I don't even like the sea that much. The critic who praises Hemingway would probably say this book has too much dialogue and not enough description. See, this story is an iceberg and you are reading the top of it. I'm hiding the bottom of the iceberg with the words I don't write. Just don't ask me about the polar bears. Because I honestly don't care. I don't drink enough to get Hemingway.

Or maybe I can write all Orwellian here and scare the hell out of you. Yeah. The government is watching every move you make, every act you do. They're controlling you and you don't even realize. You are a manipulated cockroach who lives in *The Matrix*. Just a sheep being pushed in the direction they want you to go.

Something tells me I am not the best guy for that kind of writing. I'm too much of a wiseass. Readers would view it as a comedy and laugh as I got dragged off the stage yelling, "This is not a joke! This is not a joke!"

How about if I write like Twain and use reverse psychology? Racism is bad, so for me to tell you that it's bad, I'll say a racist slur two million times to show you just how hurtful a word it can be. But it's cool, since the main character isn't racist. There is a lesson involved in the story. Then everyone will yell at me for being racist, but really I was trying to teach you all a lesson. Good job Sammy. You screwed my story with one word.

I am not going to be like Joyce either and describe every freaking crack in the road as I walk. I'll take five pages to paint a picture of the campus; I'll narrate so much of the world I live in that you'll forget that I'm telling a story. Actually, it may not be a bad idea for you to forget what I'm saying.

Or how about if I write like Kafka and not even finish this damn thing? I'll write with such pain and hopelessness that you won't even know what the hell is going on. Is this book complete? Does it have meaning? Should it have meaning? Is the meaning to it that it has no meaning? I should take from Hemingway and Kafka by writing half a book in five words and being praised for it.

Or what if I'm like Salinger or Lee and write a literary classic and just walk away. I change literature. Everyone can't wait for more from me, but they get nothing. As long as publishers don't make up bullshit reasons to produce "new original" material from me that isn't very new. I'd probably be a jerk about writing a classic too, if I ever did it. *"Yeah. That's right. I wrote the Great American Novel in one shot. How many novels did you write? No classics? Oh too bad.* At least if my friends Natacha and Paige ask me what I'm doing in between classes, I will have a great answer. *Yeah so I wrote a classic piece of literature with an iconic character and a timeless story that will be taught and inspire readers for years to come. Other than that I haven't been doing much.* I could write a classic and those two would still give me a hard time.

They could even be assigned to read a book that I wrote and still not be convinced.

No matter how I write this, it will be funny to me how this book is viewed in the future. Some will like it because of its timeless elements. Uh...yeah. I don't know what that means either. Some will dislike it since I failed to write a story that could relate to the future. My bad on that one. I haven't gone to a fortuneteller in a while and the last one I went to mentioned nothing of that. I bet this book will be forgotten in the future. Never read by anyone. Never spoken of in book clubs. Never taught in schools. I highly doubt people (no matter the time period) are interested in what I have to say. I'm honestly thinking about just taking from the writers of the past. Why not? It's better than anything I have to say.

To be honest with you, I don't like first person narratives. You know, what this is. I always preferred third person with the narrator being a secondary character, or the guy who the book is not named after of. That is obviously not the format I'm using now. I am not giving you details of another character. Nope. It's just me. Sorry. I wish I was Watson too. At least then I could be talking to Holmes and solving crimes. First person narratives rely too much on the author's tone, how witty they are, how much you're supposed to relate to them. Yeah, because the writer actually sucks at describing the scene (like Hemingway). Third person narratives are much more objective. They give me the situation without a bias and I like that. Which just adds to the sense that I am writing this in first person (it doesn't).

Since this is a first person narrative, I am the star of the book. Whether I want to be or not. That's right, me. I am the reason you'll read this, because you can relate to me and don't mind that I suck at writing descriptions. Because I get it. I get you and your life and your problems. Ah…yeah…let's go with that timeless element. Or I'll be the reason you'll stop reading this. You will find me an annoying asshole that won't shut up.

I had a history teacher in high school who didn't like my style of writing. Her name was Miss Coxman. Unfortunately for her, she was attractive, and because of her name the boys would make immature jokes behind her back about it sounding like a man's part. I wrote a paper about the American Revolution for the class. I don't even remember what the paper was on. Probably how George Washington thought America would rip itself apart from the inside. After class, she pulled me aside and said to me, "You don't write like how you speak. It's not right." And I got a D on the paper. So yeah, I'm sorry to tell you this, but you are not the first person to criticize my writing.

Miss Coxman was actually married to another history teacher, Mr. Schmidt. She kept her name because she was a teacher before she met him and didn't mind the jokes made behind her back. He was an idiot. He tried to act so cool with his clean shaved face and nice suits. He definitely watched fake late- night host like Jeremy Taits every night. My parents couldn't stand him—the teacher, not the host—because Mr. Schmidt thought he knew me better than them. How I should do this in his class, how I should do that; meanwhile, I was telling them how much of an idiot he was. Teachers think by explaining a history lesson or an equation that they all of a sudden know you better than the people who you lived with your whole life. Mr. Schmidt thought he was witty by saying dumb things like, "Don't assume. It'll make an ass out of you and me." As if it was such a great revelation. I don't know how I learned anything from that man. Those are the same type of people who use contradictions just to sound smart. I'm only up when I'm down. I only know good when I see evil. Since, up is the opposite of down. Get it? People really think they are so smart sometimes, but really they are stupid. See what I did there?

If you want to disregard my quality of writing, just think of who I am to you. Am I who you want to be or who you really are, or both? And what part of society do I represent and why? Was that conversation I had just a metaphor? Am I a metaphor? Is this whole thing a metaphor? Or is this an iceberg? Maybe the iceberg is the metaphor. I'm telling you, I should have written this in third person.

I skimmed somewhere that the greatest YA novel shouldn't be taught in the classroom, but passed around in secret by the students and read without the parents' consent. Until of course, Corporate America catches on to the popularity of the book and commercializes the idea, making it available in every bookstore and into a movie, defeating the whole ideal of the YA novel being a secret for the students in the first place. If that was the case, I am writing the greatest YA novel right now since I'll be the only one carrying around this goddamn book.

While I am giving you my opinion on writing, I might as well tell you that this is not a coming of age story where the character learns some great lesson at the end. I can't stand those types of stories. All those characters do is bitch and complain about stupid life decisions they've made. *"Oh, I overdosed. Oh, I got drunk. Oh, my friend died."* Young adult books are too much of a pity party for me. It's like the narrator wants me to feel bad for him for being an insecure moron. Yeah. That's not happening. It's called life. Get over it. And then after all the remarks, all the complaining, the character learns an important life lesson at the end. *"Now I understand more about life."* Bullshit. The author needed an ending and decided that giving you a lesson worked best. I also can't help but feel that authors are taking advantage of their young naïve audience in YA books. They know that most of their readers have probably not experienced anything they are writing about. Kids don't know much about sex or drugs or life in general. And if readers do act like they know so much, how long have they been living, twenty years, at most?

How many twenty-year-olds do you know have their act together? Not many. So YA authors write about whatever they want because their audience won't object to it anyway. And if you are old and reading a YA book, then it's time to re-examine your life. Go to a support group or something because that is just strange.

You know what's even weirder than that is the forty-five-year-old who writes about kids my age. 'Cause you know the author just gets us. He knows our way of life, how we are, even though he hasn't been to school in twenty years. Thanks for teaching me valuable life lessons that don't relate to me, moron.

And what is this new trend of YA books with the heroes being like ten years old? What the hell is up with that? You're the hero? The kid who still rides his bike around town and doesn't have a license is the person everyone is hoping will save the world? How long does it take to save the world anyway? Because according to YA authors, it takes like ten books for the ten year old kid, who is an adult by the end, to stop the evil jerk from destroying the world. The whole thing is stupid. If you haven't gone through puberty, then you shouldn't be the hero in a story. If you need people to tell you that you are the hero, then you are not the hero!

This is not a YA book because I want it to be. It is one because I am that age. Other than that, I won't make any promises about this story being an actual YA story. I'd tell you this is literary fiction, but I don't really know what that means. It's probably one of those terms that teachers came up with to better describe a book.

Also, don't expect a moral here. Hell, I'll go as far to say that you shouldn't even expect an ending. The only reason this story will end is because I can't write forever. Not because I want to inspire you or preach a lesson from the Bible.

While I'm at it, I might as well tell you this isn't a romance either. Sorry to all of those who love to read about love. I'm not going to meet the girl of my dreams and make her fall for me. Wrong book.

I just don't get modern writers. All of them. Not just YA. I really don't. All they want to do is write about unrealistic scenarios. Like a cop as the main character investigating a situation the reader will never be in, or a fantasy world filled with a large array of colorful characters and more situations the reader can't relate to. It all has purpose though. That's what writers do. We make up worlds and characters in order to teach the reader a lesson. You know because writing about the world we live in wouldn't make sense. Is the real world that boring that no one likes to write about it? Apparently all those fake images and news gets so dull that writers feel the urge to make up their own. See, that backpack is a metaphor for a bullshit lesson that the writer may or may not have been trying to tell you. If you don't know, just ask your teacher about it or read it up online. Don't worry, there is crap to describe the crap you don't understand.

Metaphors and symbols are just cheap excuses for teachers to teach the students about books that they themselves could have never written. They can't write like Twain, so they have to teach him.

Teachers ruin stories too. They overanalyze every freaking word, like the story is an artifact from a thousand years ago. They don't understand writing, so they overcomplicate it. I'm sure they don't mean to.

They have to tell the students something about the book. That is their job after all. No teacher can read a book to the class and shake their head: "I have no idea what this author is trying to say." Worst-case scenario, the teachers talk about the themes of the story so they don't look like complete fools. Because that is what students really want to hear about. Themes: that's just another way of saying lessons.

The best is when teachers give students questions about the books that they read. Do teachers really think writers write novels so that students can answer questions about them? That's totally why I'm writing this. In fact, I love questions so much I decided to write some just for this:

1. **What is the name of the book you are reading? (Are you positive about that? Check the cover, just to make sure.)**

2. Who wrote it?

3. How many pages in did you fall asleep as the teacher read this?

4. Did you really read the chapters that were assigned to you? (Admit it.)

If I liked a book in school, I could always rely on a bad teacher to lead me away from it. I wasn't like that girl in high school carrying around *The Odyssey* in my spare time. I only read what I was assigned to read, if that much.

You gotta love how writers aren't even the most influential people in literature anymore. From teachers, to publishers, to actors, my words aren't even my words.

If I ever did read this book in school, because that's going to happen (it's not), I'd probably sleep through at least a few chapters. Which means I'd get a 25% on the quiz. All of a sudden it's chapter six and the narrator is in a place I don't remember learning about and is talking to characters I don't know. In a few pages, I'd be out. All of a sudden I'd be talking to Moose. He'd wake me up in the college café. "For God's sake, man. Wake up! This is your story!"

I'd try to shake off the fact that I missed major parts of the book. "Oh sorry. The narrator was boring me."

"You are the narrator!"

"Oh."

"I told you you should pay more attention when writing."

Moose is much smarter in my imagination. In real life, he's a moron and wouldn't get this book. Yeah, that's how dumb he is. This book is over his head. At least he's not John Cage talking about some rocks.

With my luck, by the time I'm done with this book, schools would have taken all the books I mocked off of the curriculum. Goddammit! I don't care if the students learn of Atticus Finch or if they can relate to Holden Caufield, by getting rid of those books no one will get any of my jokes. The room will be silent. One wiseass student (who isn't asleep) may even mock me! "Is this guy trying to be funny? Because I don't get it." That's because the books I talked about are no longer in your classroom. How can anyone understand my jokes if all the books I joke about are not in the schools! This is why I'm becoming a comedian, not a novelist. I hate school.

And can someone please tell me why I have to write a story with a message and reason anyway? Who made up that stupid rule? People have a hard enough time finding meaning in their own lives. They don't need me to write a story for them to analyze. You are taking a lesson about life from me. Think about that for a second. It makes no sense to me either.

The only people worse than teachers are actors. Freaking actors. I hope they hate this book so that no actor ever wants to make this a film. My luck is that it will be filmed at Stage 5 Studios. Actors have such egos. It makes me want to punch them in the face every time I see one. Whenever an actor dies, I don't get sad. In fact, I don't even shed a tear: just another arrogant, self-righteous bastard dead. I know that if this book is ever made into a film (I swear to freaking God!) the interpretation of my jokes will be lost. People will think I'm not being sarcastic and like a teacher overanalyze this. But actors are worse. They'll pretend like they had a part in these words. Like they are right here next to me helping with this. *You see how he wrote this book. Mind boggling. Blah. Blah. Blah. More over thinking. I misinterpreted a book I didn't even read, give me an award.* Jackasses. All of them.

It's weird to me the different perception I will have of this story compared to you, the reader. You will read this and assume all of the people in this are characters I made up and every situation was setup for a better story. But to me, that is far from the truth. All the people and places here are real and this all really happened. Even if you think otherwise.

It just makes it hard for me to write every so often knowing the confusion we may have. To me, the biggest difference between a person and a character is that people have lives, while characters have stories. If nothing happens for three weeks in a story the writer can go ahead three weeks in his story with the words, *"Three weeks went by."* But a person can't do that. I can't do that. You can't do that. If their life isn't exciting, they can't go forward and talk about only the juicy stuff. Living a life isn't the same as being in a story.

I'm not sure if I explained that well. Anyway at this point, you may be asking yourself just why exactly I'm writing this. Good question. I bet you are the type of person who doesn't even need the SparkNotes version of a book. I'm not writing this so it can capture a time and a people. Sorry to teachers like Mr. Richard out there. I wish I could have these words mean something too. I believe you are looking for a real writer. He'll show up a little later with his book for you to sign.

This whole story, if you want to call it that—I just call it a long digression but whatever—is probably not as fascinating as I think it is. Don't quote me on this, but I'm pretty sure my story would be more interesting if I had a mental breakdown or if I fought a dragon. Maybe I could fight a dragon as I had a mental breakdown. Maybe. I'm actually thinking about lying about this whole thing just to add some flavor to it. Believe it or not, there is a reason I am writing all of this. I'm lying, I mean, I'm writing this because my comedy instructor told the class that the only way to improve at writing is to write. Everyday. For at least an hour. Which is just way too much writing for me to do. So I decided to write this. Whatever this is. Yet another reason I love teachers.

You probably have no idea who the instructor is for my comedy class. Don't worry. I didn't even know him before signing up for it either. His name is James Marson. Besides being behind the reason I am writing this, he is a successful comedian. He does it for a living, which I found hard to believe at first. If I saw the guy in a supermarket just casually looking for chips, I would not guess comedian; definitely fat guy, but not comedian. After hearing that he knew comedians like Jeremy Taits, Lenny Small, and Randy Landfield, I began to see him as a man who can actually do comedy. He doesn't care how he looks and you can tell; from his overweight body to his unshaved face, appearance is not a trait that is high with this guy. He gives us pretty good advice at the beginning of each class as he leans on the back of his chair. That's how he teaches us. A few words in the beginning and then the ten of us (or however many are there) go up on stage for five minutes each and do our routine. He comments on each bit after each of us is done, like what the host at open mic does, just Marson knows what he's talking about. His beginning of class advice is more helpful than anything he told me after I performed. Stuff like, "Hide behind humor. If anyone ever gets offended, tell them it was a joke. Drama can't do that." He also said to create a persona. The person you are on the stage should be able to sell. He went as far to say that some of us should change our names to fit our personas. That wasn't it for his tips either. He mentioned that a person should be able to laugh regardless of the actual content of the joke. He used the example of a comedian who joked about being set on fire. He asked us, "How many of you have ever been set on fire?" Luckily none of us raised our hands. "And yet this is still a funny routine because it wasn't about being set on fire. You could relate to it for other reasons. Do you understand what I'm saying?" That was the most explaining Marson would do for the class. I'll definitely follow one of those pieces of advice. Which means that I probably won't.

The name of the club where the class takes place is called *The Scraper* because it's located in the city with skyscrapers that the tourists love to take pictures of. The title always has to relate to whatever the hell the thing is about; you'll see stuff like that whenever you go to a place or read a book or whatever. It's kind of an unwritten rule in life. You can't make it in the world if you give your shit a random name. It has to be a pun or a witty reference that society could understand. You will fail if you don't do this. I'd like to imagine that the owner of the club was just walking past all the bums and lights in the city when one day it all clicked. "Skyscrapers are all around here. If I get rid of the word *sky* and add the word *the,* I can have a name for my comedy club." And the dumb name for the club was born. We don't appreciate stupid brilliance like that enough.

The place is really nice too. Way too nice for amateurs who can barely tell a joke. It's even cleaner than the white corridor in the science building at school. Probably because it doesn't have as many pamphlets. As soon as you walk in there's a red carpet that leads to the main room, which is where the class goes in, besides that one time the class was downstairs, which is where the open mic takes place every Wednesday night. That room is a hellhole. You can't take a step without falling off the stage. The lights are too bright and the room is on an angle so the stage is in the corner, not the middle of the room. The architect designing the room clearly didn't care about the future open mics the place may have. Add to that an idiot host and you got yourself one of the worst open mics in the city. The guy is a nobody in comedy, yet he has the balls to tell others what is wrong with their jokes. Marson can do that. He's a professional. He gets paid to do it. Who is this guy? Nobody, that's who. He sits there with his pen and clipboard as if he's doing such a hard job watching comedy and announcing who is next up on stage. One time his advice for a comedian was to change the time frame in his bit. I'm not joking. The MC told the guy that instead of saying an event happened five hundred years ago, he should say it happened seven hundred years ago. That's the type of feedback you expect at an open mic. Awful, pointless feedback. Guys like the MC can insult anyone but when it comes for his time to go on stage, he sucks. More than Miss Coxman. Oh man, that was mean. Not because the open mic host is talented. He's not. Now if I said that the open mic host at *The Scraper* sucked like Cherry Lovin, then I may be right. She gets around. As far as I know, Miss Coxman is a faithful wife. Even if it is to an idiot like Mr. Schmidt. The open mic host at *The Scraper* means so little to me that I didn't even bother remembering his freaking name.

Luckily for the class, we perform in the main room, which can fit about one-fifty or so, has a stage you can dance on, and the lighting isn't so bad. None of us sit at the tables, but by the half-booths facing the stage, so it's comfortable to be there even if the comedy may suck.

On the wall as soon as you walk into the club is a bunch of black and white pictures of comedians from the past. Randall, Jeremy Taits, and Lenny Small all have a picture on the wall that comedians would put in the newspaper to promote their shows. They either have that look of a person who is surprised they are taking a picture or they are just smiling. I recognize some of the faces of the comedians, like the ones I told you, but I can't put a name to some of them. I've seen them on TV or in a movie but I was never a fan. It would be funny if a few were not even in comedy. Like they are the club's janitor or a teacher. There are too many pictures on the wall for me to count them. What? Do you think I'm counting the pictures on the wall as soon as I walk in? Really? While I'm at it, I might as well act like a talkative New Yorker and say hello to the guy at the door and inform him that I am only there to count the pictures on the wall. I don't care for the class being taught or the open mics. I'm there for the pictures.

Most times there is a guy actually at the door. His name is Jake. He's a couple years older than me. I went to *Roncho's Lounge* with him a few times until it got too packed for me. He may still go. It has been about a week or two since the last time we went. He performed a bunch of impressions of actors and famous people for his routine. The thing about him that's so different is that he's smart. I don't know many smart people. Most I come across are pretty dumb. He's one of the few that talks like he went to school. The drunk on the train would like him. Some people talk like they're idiots. All they do is ramble on and curse and hope that by saying a few witty comments, you will think they have some intelligence. It's like they are trying to show you they are fools. I wonder what the hell Jake is even doing in comedy if he has a brain. Aren't there polar bears to save or something? I'm pretty sure there are people in other nations having their human rights taken from them. Don't those people need help?

He isn't in the class, just works at the club as a teller. His job is to allow people in and out of the club. Whenever I show up to class, I see him. We know each other enough by now that when I show up he just lets me in. He knows why I'm really there. The pictures on the wall. Sometimes I go for the low-priced beer too. I don't really know if there's a security guard at the club. I've never seen a guard when I walked in. It makes sense to only have a guy like Jake be the authoritative figure in the club. I'm sure a fat white guy with glasses and an overbite is really going to scare all those terrorists out there. The guys at Dairy Barn shake when they see Jake. I do too. He's really ugly.

I'm not sure if you know who he is, but in the comedic world Randy Landfield is a big name. His approval is everything for us newcomers who have a hard enough time getting up on stage. He has made people's careers by giving them a thumbs-up and letting them perform at his nightclub, *Randall's*. Here's the thing about his club though: no open mics. Guys like me are not allowed to perform there just to improve or to hang out with some buddies from class. The Pun Guy is not allowed on stage. The Book Reader is never shown the door. None of my classmates perform there. You have to earn a place at *Randall's*. You have to prove that you are funny and can be a professional comedian. The catch is that you are expected to do that at other open mics. There are even sayings about Randy's influence over the field. *"If Randy likes you, soon everyone will." "All careers begin with Randy."* Marson included those lines in the folder he gave us on the first day of class. You don't make it in comedy without meeting Randall. Actors, stand-ups, talk-show hosts, all can be traced back to getting a chance at his club. If he ever sees me at an open mic and likes my act, then I could actually have a career with humor. That's how big Randall Landfield is.

From what I know of his comedic career, Landfield is done with comedy. He doesn't tour, go on late night shows, or show his face as much as he used to ten years ago or so. Now he is focused on running his club and finding new young comedic talent. He was a big dog in his day. Popular enough to get his own club, I mean. I can't really tell you much about the guy's personal life, if he's married, if he ever got divorced, since I honestly never really looked into it myself. If he's anything like other comedians, he definitely has skeletons in the closet.

I can't even tell you how many comedians I've heard of that were beloved as comedians, but messed up as people. I'm convinced my story is the least interesting one you'll read. The best example of a famous yet questionable comedian that I know of is Craig Deanimo. He's an old time comedian. An eccentric man known for acting so silly in films that you had to laugh. He hung himself at the age of forty-eight. During his life he had four marriages, including one to a nineteen-year-old, was a misogynistic racist who beat the women he was with, and served time in jail for several reasons: domestic abuse, DWI, drugs, and public disturbance. Apparently his stand up was so outrageous at times that he got hauled off for the night. He was a drunk, had depression, and has been quoted on numerous occasions for saying things that would make you second-guess what country he supports. And yet when you talk about comedy icons, he's someone that is always brought up. He is the guy we think of when we mention humor. Look up laughter and this guy's face will pop up. Funny how that works out.

Then there's Jeremy Taits, a popular talk show host. Been on the air for eight to ten years now. He has a gambling problem and likes to spend his off time at strip clubs and casinos. He divorced his wife of fifteen years after he cheated on her with a younger co-worker. Although I would guess it was the other way around, with the divorce, I mean. You wouldn't know his true behavior by his late night persona. Everyone wants to be on his show. Athletes, actors, scientists, politicians: they all love being interviewed by him. He has a good-guy look to him: clean shave, short hair, good smile. You would never associate him with a sly, cheating, addict son of a bitch. Everyone loves his show. To him, though his show is just that: a show.

The funniest situation is Daniel Isles. He's a comedian who stills tours the country. Still a pretty big name in comedy. If you and your friends hear that he is at the local comedy club, one of them may show interest. You may not go, but you know who he is and will think about going for a second. Of course, his popularity is not from his standup career alone. It helped that he was the nice guy on a family comedy that was on the air for ten years. It ended about seven years ago or so. Don't take my word on that. I was never a fan of the show. In it, Isles was the moral character that tried to create peace and love between the friends. He would often have a lesson to get out of every odd scenario he was in. Like some bullshit lesson about working hard and having a good character. And if you go to see this guy, the first joke out of his mouth is about fellatio. The whole night is filled with curses and dirty jokes. He is a different person on stage than in the show and people are upset by that. I even heard him a few times in interviews defending his standup, "Look I was acting. When I'm onstage doing comedy, I'm not acting." How is that for a joke? One of the most honorable TV characters was played by a crude pervert.

Like all classes, there is a teacher's pet. A student that the teacher loves and embraces as if they were family. Harry Bent is his name. I only know his full name because he was also outside the main room when Carl, another classmate, told us about the inspiration behind his comedic career. I remember thinking to myself that Bent is a really unusual last name to have. My last name is Cripp, so I know about head-scratching last names. My family is actually convinced that it was somehow shortened in the past. So much so that snooty German-speaking professors can't even figure out my ethnicity.

How do I explain Harry's type of comedy? Oh boy, that's a tough question. Well for starters, it isn't really comedy in the traditional sense. He doesn't just get up on stage and tell jokes. "Hey folks, have you heard the one about the school?" Comedy has a three- step rule: beginning, setup, and punch line. I only learned that from a slip of paper in that folder I got on the first day of class. The one that mentioned about *Randall's*. For a few pieces of paper it sure said a lot. More than any of those awful YA books with vampires and wizards. No offense to any writers who like that sort of stuff. Harry doesn't really fit into that traditional comedy mold. What's his style? I really don't know. I'll just tell you about what he did and let you decide. Once he just stood up on stage for five minutes, not saying a word. He just stood there with the microphone in hand and stared at us in the audience. Seriously, that was his act. He didn't look around or move. He just focused his eye on the back wall and waited. Another time he took out a gun and pretended to shoot himself. He didn't wait five minutes for that odd routine. No. He got up on stage and adjusted the mic, which is the first thing comedians do when they get up on stage. The mic is never set in a place the comedian is comfortable with so he or she moves it. Sometimes the comedian even takes it off the stand. It depends. I'm not sure why I am telling you about that. It is as interesting as the newspaper club.

With his microphone in hand Harry said to us, "I have something to say." Then he took out a fake gun, put the gun to his left ear, and fell to the ground. For the next four minutes or so he just laid there. Another time he turned his back on us and spoke to the wall. But not in English, Spanish, Swedish, or any language that I know. I can't believe I'm even saying this, but one time he stripped nude as if he was a woman on a video you would see on the web. I can't make that up. Harry got up and took his clothes off. Luckily for all of us, Marson stopped him before he got to revealing all of himself. I don't need to see that. Nobody does.

So what does Marson think of Harry? Is he ready to throw him out of class? Does he think he's an idiot? Nope. It's the opposite. Marson loves him. After every routine he has nothing but praise for him.

According to the professional, the best comedian in our class is the one who doesn't even perform comedy. Looks like someone is getting the Hemingway treatment, and it isn't me.

I don't like Harry, probably because he's a kiss-ass to Marson and nothing like my favorite comedian, Lenny Small. The comedian's real name was Leonard Smallson but he went by his stage name Lenny Small. I bet cause it sounded cooler. He was an asshole, I admit, but he was so smart that you couldn't help but respect his observations on the world. At some points in his comedy you didn't know if he was kidding or not. You'd say to yourself, "Wait, is he really joking right now? Or...what's going on?" And by then he was on to the next observation you never even thought about. He always had something to say. You may not always have agreed with him, but he did have a reason for his thinking. He was not an idiot, unlike Harry. Probably was the only comedian that could curse and still come across as a genius. Whenever someone curses, my respect for them goes down. Can't the person talk without saying fuck or shit every other word? Does that really add to the story that much that the person has to include it? Having said that, Lenny Small wrote a memoir called *"Fuck You. I Never Liked You Anyway"* about his life in comedy and all that crap fans would want to read about someone they love. It included all of his comedic material, which is a lot since he did it for forty years or so, and spanned from just about any topic you could think of, from religion, school, the English language, and buying food, to the end of the world. Lenny Small spoke of just about anything. He died a few years ago. Not tragically or anything, just of age. He never wrote a novel though. I would have liked to read what he had to say in story form. That was part of his problem, if you want to call it that. He wasn't a very good storyteller or actor. The screenplays he wrote were awful and he couldn't act. I try my best to avoid his acting roles as much as I do class. All he could do was perform his jokes. For as smart as he was, he had little impact on the world outside of comedy. I know I shouldn't let that bother me since I never met the guy, but I always had a problem with that.

Getting back to my classmates, there was one woman in the class who was actually funny. Seriously, she was. At least I thought so. She had the demeanor of a woman who had three kids and was married for ten years and just didn't care if what she said was right or not. She'd make fun of missionaries like Miss Wello and the green people. There was no persona with her. She joked about what she saw. She had one joke about emojis that I thought was really funny. It went something like, "Yeah. I see a lot of people are using emojis today. I remember learning about them when I was a kid. They were called hieroglyphics."

I may have messed up the joke. Anyway, she was smart and had enough of a sense of humor to be a real comedian, but that bit I repeated was from one of the only times she attended class. One of the few comedians in the class with good comedic skills dropped. Go figure. I bet she saw the price and ran. Hundreds of dollars for a folder must not be worth it for her.

She and Harry aren't the only two in the class. Far from it. There's Marvin. He's a bald black guy who talks real smooth. Even when he's unfunny, he still acts like he's hysterical, like he has everything under control. Doesn't move much while on the stage either. He's all head motions. You can't tell if he's trying to pick up a woman or be a comedian when he's up there. He tells jokes about never doing comedy and his job as a truck driver. The more you listen to him, the more you are relieved that he has another job.

There's an older woman like sixty or so. She's just plain creepy. Like she needs to see someone about some problems she's having. Whenever I see her at an open mic she says hi as if she is excited to see me and we're great friends that go back twenty years. Every time she talks a piece of her flaky face falls off. She definitely lives with cats. I'd say she is as attractive as the con woman in Penn Station. I talk to the Cat Lady when I see her, but I don't get any further than that because she is too weird for me. Like she'd read this and love it and find nothing wrong with it. Heck she may even carry around a copy in her pocketbook. That is the type of weird I am talking about. For a change, I don't think I am wrong for not wanting to talk to her.

Let's see, there's Carl, the fat guy who has a notebook full of jokes. That's what he told a few of us before we started the class one time, when we were waiting to enter the main room. Not that he was fat, that he had a notebook full of jokes. Apparently this guy collected all the jokes he wrote and decided to start a comedy career. He mentioned how Lenny Small inspired him to do so since he learned that's what the legendary comedian did. Carl may be Spanish or white or maybe even Greek (although I've never seen him at the Greek restaurant in town). I'm not sure what he is. He's definitely human. I mean, most likely. I know that his story of his notebook sounds like the beginning of a great career from a legendary comic. It does. But it isn't this guy's, since all Carl does is jump around and yell while on stage. Don't get me wrong, it's impressive for such a large man to move around so much, but he's not very funny. After a minute of him jumping around, you're wondering how much more time is left.

Then there is Dimitri. He's very tall and thin and dresses like he only listens to reggae music, to the point where I'd be surprised if he ever thought about wearing a suit. Before every class he's always talking to Marson about comedy, as if he is also a professional comedian. Like he's teaching a class at one of the other clubs. He's not. He's really not that great, but you wouldn't know that by how he spoke of his previous comedic experience. *Have you heard how tough the Trenton crowd is? Boy, I had a tough set last week.* I could never tell if Marson was just being nice to him, or whether he actually thought Dimitri was a respectable comedian. One time me, him, his girlfriend, and Doug grabbed a bite after class at the restaurant next door. Marson was performing at *The Scraper* later that night so we decided to stick around and see him. The show started only an hour after the class, so we didn't have to wait long. It was supposed to teach us what being a comedian was like. I think. Maybe. I just enjoyed the night. I honestly only went because I thought it was cool to watch a comedian I knew, not because I am great friends with any of my classmates. As for Dimitri, if only he was as funny as he was kind. The guy has been doing this for ten years now and has nothing to show for it. I guess he just can't take the hint.

One guy in the class whose name I don't remember because he hasn't shown up in a while dressed in a different outfit every time he went on stage. He claimed he wanted to find his style and thought that wearing different clothes each set would help. First was jeans and a t-shirt, then a suit and tie, then office attire, then he went with themes: nerdy, hood-like. And then he stopped showing up. He said he's a stay-at-home dad who thought comedy would help him. I don't know with what exactly, but that's what he said, so whatever. Keep in mind when these other comedians talk, I go in and out listening to them. Partly because they bore me and partly because I'm more worried about myself, not them. That was actually advice from Marson too.

I'm not the only young person in the class. Jesse and her friend are around my age. I don't know what compelled either of them to try standup. I bet they just love to write an hour a day. They're awful. I get them confused sometimes since they look alike with their long black hair and skinny hips. They both dress like they only realized that they had a class where they were required to be in front of people when it was too late, so they threw on whatever worn outfit they could find. I don't remember Jesse's friend's name or a routine she did while on stage. She must be pretty bad. Or I'm an idiot. Either way, Jesse has a funny habit of never telling more than one joke at a time. She'll say one and then tilt the microphone on the side, wait a second and go, "So… yeah." That's the funniest part of her routine, if you want to call it that.

Despite being the only two other classmates my age, I never really spoke to them.

I guess the closest person I can call my friend in the class is Doug. He's about forty and has a very self-deprecating comedy style: how he's too fat, how he's too bald, how his first marriage sucked, how he has no money. I've chatted with him at a few open mics. Not for the same reason as with the Cat Lady, but because I enjoy his company. There's a realness about him that I like. As I say that, he once told me how he wants to be a talk show host. He loves comedy and dreams of having his own show with his own guests. Talk show hosts are the fakest people out there. I laugh at how fake they are with their makeup and suit and tie. They pretend to like their guests and relate to the audience. Jeremy Taits acts like a character on his own show, more than a real person. I don't have the balls to tell Doug about how he will never make a good talk show host. He'll never pretend to be someone he's not. Which sucks for him, since that seems to be the norm today. Doug is more likeable than Harry. Neither are that funny. Too bad for Doug, Harry is the sexy pick. The one that they can use in press releases to promote the show, the one they can put on billboards across the city right below the musical signs. They can give off a better appearance for the network and sell more tickets with Harry as the guy. There are two people for the show. One is a forty-five-year-old balding overweight man and the other is a twenty-five-year-old slim, well-built man.

Who do you think will make it? And as for me? Oh, who the hell knows where I am in all of this.

I have noticed a genuine problem that I have with my standup. I don't care what the audience thinks. Whether they laugh or not. I really have no interest in if they think I'm funny. I tell the jokes I like and if the audience doesn't like them, then sucks for them. They can watch Harry or Doug or whatever comedian they enjoy. The laughter of the audience doesn't make me want to get back out on stage. I don't have the enthusiasm I thought I would have for this when I started.

Who will make it out of all these comedians? Will any of us be performing at *Randall's* one day to you and your buddies on a Saturday night? Or be a talk show host and joke about the latest celebrity gossip, or be an actor and star in your favorite comedy? Probably not. The one who becomes popular will be the one who kisses the most ass. So basically Harry. It also means that my chances are slim to none. I'm not the friendly type who can make conversation and make friends. I barely keep the ones I have. If you actually think you can make it in the comedic world without knowing someone then you're an idiot. It has nothing to do with your talent. I don't care what the open mic hosts tell you or what you learn in class. It is all about who you know. You're lying to yourself if you think otherwise.

Part 2 – Home 1

Most days I look like shit. Today wasn't much different. I always tell myself lies about how I will work out more or look better. I'm great at making plans in my head, coordinating the steps I'd need to be successful, but I'm not that good at following them. In that moment, my plan is the best thing ever. The idea is revolutionary and will change the world. Until it sits in a pile on the floor in my room with other "great plans" I've come up with and one day I learn that the idea wasn't so original after all. Someone much smarter than me and more determined and organized created it. If this story is not found in a pile in my room, I'd be surprised.

Yeah, even when I look good, I look bad. I have so much black under my eyes from lack of sleep you'd think that I was emo. I look like I am ready to kill someone when I'm exhausted (which is more often than not). It is funny to me since I'm not that pessimistic of a person but people who don't know me and only see my exhaustion may confuse it for anger. *Oh no, that guy may blow up a school. He may shoot this place up.* I swear I've never even thought about doing such crazy things. I just looked pissed off when I'm tired.

What makes my already appealing appearance even worse is that I hate getting haircuts. I never did like sitting in the barber chair as a stranger cuts my hair, using those absurd tools to be precise with my hair follicles. I sit there hoping the guy doesn't go all Van Gogh on me, and when it is over, I'm always asked how I think it looks. Like I know anything about that. Because now I'm an expert in fashionable hairstyles after sitting in a raised chair for five minutes. A few times I've gone in to get a haircut and told the guy it was awesome only to get home and realize it was awful. That was when I went a bunch. Now I will only get like two or three haircuts a year. That is how much I hate it. I wait for the black stuff to all grow out and then one day I get rid of it all. I just got a haircut last week at the place in town, so you can call yourself lucky that you won't see me in a few months. As for the little facial hair I have now, I am just too lazy to shave everyday. I can barely wake up on time, yet you expect me to shave each day? I do the same thing with that. One day I have a nest under my chin, then the next day I am fully cleaned. It's just easier for me to not pay any attention to my hair or looks in general.

Talking about waking up, I didn't have a good sleep last night. Which, the more I think about it, is more normal than it should be for me. At least once a week, I am up all night just staring at my ceiling as I lie in bed. I guess that explains my black eyes. Those are long days after not sleeping.

Sometimes my mind can't stop racing at night. I pace around my room trying to calm down, but I can't. I keep overthinking the whole night; should I try to get some rest, or work on some new material since my brain is already going? On one hand, my mind is ready to work, but I know that if I stay awake I will probably pass out later in the day during class, which is something I'd like to avoid. And if I go to bed right away, I miss out on a chance to use the adrenaline I built from my anxiety to write some material, or something. Adrenaline, it turns out, is not easy to come by.

I haven't told my family or friends about my sleeping problems because what is there to really tell? I don't sleep enough? That I have bad dreams? I don't see what there is to really talk about so I keep it to myself. My room is in the basement of the house, so when I can't sleep, no one in the family knows about it anyway.

They do know about the crickets in the basement that can keep me up all night. How can they not? With that annoying sound those things make, everyone hears them. I have a great method for getting those loud critters to shut up: a dictionary. Oh yeah, I get them in a place that I can place the dictionary over them and BAM! No more noises. Until I hear five more later that night. Freaking crickets. I swear if I go to hell, it will be just me sitting in a room full of crickets. Somehow when the apocalypse happens, the crickets will not go extinct, just so they can annoy the rest of nature. It's sad to say that bashing crickets it the most I have ever used a dictionary.

The light switch in both rooms, the bathroom and my bedroom, are cracked from when I punched them awhile back. I probably just needed to punch something at the time. Everyone gets that way every so often. You just want to hit something because you are that pissed off at life. You failed a test, didn't get the girl. Whatever it was, you failed. You should have a way to get your anger out that is socially acceptable. It may be the only thing that could keep you from going nuts. And if you never show any anger at anything in your life, then I suggest consulting your local pastor because that's not right. As someone I know always says, "Some things in this world should piss you off. If they don't, then what the hell are you doing?" I don't remember why I got so aggravated. I don't normally get mad at anything. I'd go as far to say that I am probably the calmest person you'll ever meet. I'm so laid back, you would think I do drugs. I don't though, in case you were wondering. When I get angry my family and friends are shocked. I'm good at keeping my cool. Must be all the Buddhism I'm reading. My fit was probably over some small stupid thing, like I spilled soda on some paper on the floor, or the dirt from my shoes got all over the place. Want to drive someone mad? Do some minor thing like change around their desk or sit in their seat when they are tired. They'll flip. When the little things in life don't go people's way, they lose it.

As soon as I woke up this morning and got out of bed, I nearly fell. Not because I'm a klutz, but because of all the damn paper on the floor in my room. Sometimes I forget I even have a floor. I'm used to the mess at this point. All the papers on the floor are from

comedy class and school and other random stuff I
failed to organize. I'm the worst at keeping track of
my things. I'm surprised I haven't lost anything yet.
For you, a successful story consists of a good plot,
well-developed characters, and a good voice. To me, a
successful story is one I can find the next day.

When I got out of my room, I staggered over to the
bathroom. The laundry room lights were on and I
could hear someone loading and unloading clothes. I
greeted whoever it was in my family that was up
before me with a simple, "Hey." That's the most I can
muster early in the morning. Before I heard a
response, I saw it was my mom doing the laundry
dressed for work in her gym teacher sports attire.
She's been one as long as I can remember. I'm unsure
whose clothes she was doing exactly. There seems to
be a never-ending battle my family has with the
laundry. It's never done. Just when we have all the
baskets empty and organized, someone drops a pile
of dirty clothes all over the small room. The only thing
less rewarding than the completion of laundry is the
emptying of the dehumidifier next to the laundry. We
have to change that thing like ten times a day.

"I found your phone in your pants." You can tell she
was already wide-awake, unlike me. She must have
had some coffee upstairs.

"Thanks. I was looking for it." I wasn't.

"Nick, make sure to carry your phone with you."
People still use the excuse of *"in case of an emergency"* to carry their phones around with them. Yeah, and what do they do on their phone? Play games and watch porn. That sure sounds like an emergency to me. What would I do without another repetitive colorful addictive game or another video of a hot chick getting naked in front of a camera? That's what the world needs more of: stupid mobile games and porn. Things that can really help people.

Don't even talk to me about porn. It's bullshit. They have actors pretend to fulfill some sort of fantasy you have. All I see when I watch porn are deprived individuals who are so messed up that they enjoy that crap. Well I see that most of the time. You think the world is fucked up? You're right. There are people out there making money off your orgasms.

Whenever you bring up porn or adult dating sites to college students, they all say no, they know nothing about them. And they all go to church every Sunday and would never let temptation get the best of them since they are such angels. They study for all their classes and never curse. Yeah, sure. That's what's so funny about porn. No one wants to admit to watching it, at least no one I know. Which is pretty easy today since every other song, video, and commercial has a sexual innuendo. I can't stand when it's early in the morning and the first thing I hear on the radio is a song about a guy trying to bang a hot chick and then the radio show talks of sexual problems and the commercials have sexual innuendos in them. Really world, is that how perverted we all have become? We can't go a day without innuendo in our culture. I was watching a commercial like that, the other morning before I went to school, before I was even awake. I didn't even have a cup of coffee at that time. You can't sell sex to a guy who hasn't had his coffee; it's not fair. In the video, there was a woman and a repairman. The guy says, "Oh, you want it hard?" And the woman responds, "You know I want it really hard." Then the guy takes out a hammer or some tool, even though we totally know they were talking about his dick. The commercial goes to a screen telling me how durable the product is. Even when you're not watching porn, you're watching porn. Don't call me Orwell, but that is a definite feature I would include if I wanted to manipulate a society.

Thanks to those adult sites, I have a date tonight. Well, more like a planned hookup, but for now let's call it a date. Look, I admit it, I signed up for one of those bullshit sites where they get you by preying on your temptations. It was a dumb decision. One minute, there is a picture of a naked woman on my phone and the next I'm messaging a real woman to hookup. I can't believe she said yes to me. Must be the beautiful mug I sent her. I didn't upload my actual picture on the profile page because I feel insecure about it. But I am fine with being on an adult site, that's made for hookups with strangers for some reason. Her name is Molly and she had a few suggestive pictures on her profile and after some messaging back and forth we agreed to only do it if we met in a public place. She didn't want me to be a crazy rapist or stalker. She might not be too happy to find out I'm an asshole, but at least I'm not a rapist.

I'm kind of surprised she even said yes to meeting up. Why? I guess I'm taken back that someone even wants to meet me. I'll be honest with you; I don't even want to meet myself. I don't know what I would do if I saw myself the way the world sees me. That's an event I wouldn't mind missing. Maybe it's the same reason I hate hearing my own voice. The voice in my head sounds better.

If you think that me going to meet her is unusual, then you should hear about the last girl I met in the city. I've used the Internet to meet various people before. Once I met an Asian woman in the city for dinner. We met at this upscale Japanese restaurant in the city and I wore a blue t-shit with a squirrel on it making a joke about nuts. Why did I wear such inappropriate attire? Because I wanted to see if this woman would hate me for being me. If I have to change to hang out with you, then I don't want to be with you. I'm not paying to be your friend and I'm not changing either. And I was right. She hated me for wearing such an outfit. We only met online, so it wasn't like we were exactly upscale citizens ourselves. Halfway through the meal she told me how she had no job and how she went on other dates like the one we were on. It occurred to me that she was using her first dates as a way to eat. She knew the man would pay, (or at least, he would most likely pay) so she got a free meal out of it. Her plan worked too. I paid for both of our meals and we never saw each other after that. We didn't even exchange numbers.

I'm not as into video games as much I used to be (which is as bad of a segue as I could have come up with). Growing up, all I did was play video games. Matt and I would play late into the night, and then I'd go home and play more games. I blame my reading deficiencies on video games. If you think I have limited writing abilities, then blame the generation of video games I grew up with. In fact, I am wondering why I didn't mock video games to start this instead of literature. Something about an hour. I know more about them than literature.

Now, I can't tell what's the game and what's life. They're too realistic, if you ask me. I don't get the appeal of playing a game as if it's real. Why is it cool to see the veins in the person's body, or the pores in their skin? Games weren't like that when Matt and I played them. They were silly and animated. You knew you were playing in a made-up universe. Besides, I have my own life to worry about. I don't need another life that isn't even real. Thanks, but no thanks.

I think both porn and video games want controversy so they can be in the spotlight. Porn wants religious groups to yell at them. Video game creators want to be discussed as a source of shooters' inspiration. Even me stupidly telling you how I feel about them is putting spotlight on them. Which is just what they want, 'cause if they're on your mind, it means something else isn't. A lot of other industries have adopted this mindset too. Just turn on the news and you'll see what I mean. They'll report a scandal just to remind you they exist. It's like staring at a car accident. You know you shouldn't, but you're oddly intrigued. Is watching porn really a sin? Did that killer shoot up the school because of that game? Was that driver drunk? All topics that a philosophy teacher may bring up eventually in class. I don't know about you, but I can't wait for that day. Gonna have to make sure I'm early to that class. Actually, he may have even assigned some homework on one of those topics. Never mind.

I answered my mom, who was just about done with the laundry, with my usual sarcasm. Ever see someone wear a shirt about being sarcastic all the time? That's me. I know that you probably think everyone says that who's sarcastic, but I mean it. Or do I? Maybe I'm just being sarcastic about my sarcasm.

"But if I bring my phone, that'll encourage people to call me."

She was used to my tone by now. "Just bring it with you," she said without looking up. "I'm going to Mari's wake tonight. Dad has a meeting. Renee and Kate have classes." They are my sisters. "We'll all be home late, so you're on your own for dinner." On my own normally means cereal or fast food or leftovers since the fridge is only filled with condiments like ketchup and salsa. No real food. Just the stuff that goes with real food. "There's leftover Chinese food in the fridge if you want it." That answered my dinner plans.

What is my dad's meeting about? What classes are my sisters taking? Oh come on! Don't do that to me! I don't see my family much since I started going to college because we are all either out or working or at classes. When we do see each other, it's a quick conversation like the one I had with my mom. While I'm at it, I might as well tell you about things I know a lot about. Like art and pons and Kelvin. I may even change this whole story, just to make it about people that I like.

I don't know who this Mari woman was and Mom didn't explain because she was too busy with the laundry. I just assumed it was a friend of hers from school. Want to get a good laugh? My mom is a teacher and my two sisters Kate and Renee are becoming teachers. My dad is not a teacher. He works in an office. I can't stand when people talk about other people as if you should know who they are. They will have full- blown conversations talking about the person and not once describe them or anything. And why? People assume you know them, which you don't. *Hey have you heard about George? Can you believe that he did that? I can't. The way he behaved when we were out last time, ridiculous. That's George being George though.* When I hear people talk like that I just want to stand up and shout at them, "No, I don't know what you're talking about! Who the hell is George?" There is no easy way to tell someone who thinks you know what they're talking about that you have no idea what they're talking about. It's best to go along and hope they change topics. Maybe they will talk about their niece becoming a music teacher, or their kid going to a costume party. Something you're not really interested in either, but at least you can follow along with their digression.

Want to hear another thing funny? The most people to ever gather in one place just for you will be at your wake. Think about that: when else will hundreds of people go out of their way at that same time just for you?

I have some experience with this stuff. Like, I know that the funeral home gives away these plastic cards the size of a coupon with a sappy poem on it. If you weren't heartbroken and in tears, you'd ridicule this poem, or even ignore it entirely, but you are aching, so the shallow prose will do. Imagine being the author of that poem when you learn that your work is used at funerals. I guess it's cool? It must be nice that people are reading your work. It may not be the best situation, but hey, it's better than an open mic, so there is that. If you never had the luxury of going to a wake then you have no idea what I'm talking, but you'll see. The funeral home has hundreds of these cards for the person that died. On one side of the card is the aforementioned beautiful verse and on the other side is a picture of something that is meant to make you feel better. Like Jesus or a beach.

I told my mom my plans for the day, which consisted of fun stuff like going to school—woo-hoo, go education—and I wished her to have a good day, which would be difficult since she'd be at a wake and all, but it couldn't hurt.

"Don't forget to go to the University Center to get your sticker for your car." I'd forgotten, because I was clearly focused on all my schoolwork, obviously. Each car on campus has to have a parking sticker. No sticker and you will get ticketed. And I mean every car on campus. Even the teachers need it.

"Thanks," I said. Moms will always be moms.

Always thinking about how I may slip on a paper on the floor, get into a car accident, or be late for class. I think it's impossible for moms to be calm. I grabbed a towel from the rack and went into the bathroom to take a shower.

After all that I didn't even take my phone.

Let me ask you a stupid question: is it normal to pass out in the shower? You don't have to answer that. But I will tell you that I do sometimes. I put on the hot water and I feel really dizzy, sit down, and then I just fall over. All of a sudden, some time has passed and

I'm still in the hot shower. It only occurs in hot water. It must be the steam or something. I don't know. I'm no scientist, but I can't stay in a hot shower for too long. At least, I can't stay in it awake. When I'm not passing out, I am, you know, taking an actual shower.

After I got out of the shower, I put on my clothes. A very eccentric and revealing look, my blue jeans, gray t-shirt, and my black jacket. What can I say about my fashion? Other than I have none? What should make you worry more than the dullness of my appearance is that I will probably be wearing just as plain of an outfit tomorrow. I've heard people say that colors can reflect your attitude on life, or whatever. I don't pay much attention to it when I hear such information that's supposed to enlighten me, since my look says nothing interesting about me. I changed in the middle of the downstairs basement since everyone in the family was gone by then.

I practiced some of my jokes as I walked upstairs. Which went as well as you think it went, in that it didn't go well at all. Jokes only appear funny in my head as thoughts, but then I write them down and realize that they kind of suck.

I popped some bread in the toaster and then sat down to write. Toast is the only food I can make. Besides cereal, but that's not a food to me as much as a separate food group altogether. I'm quite the cook and offer a variety of the toast delicacy: burnt toast, brown toast, raw toast, toast with butter, toast with cream cheese. I am what you would call a toast expert.

I didn't turn on the radio because there's only so much of that nonsense I can take. Half of what is said is a contradiction, just a story, a filler. Whether any of it has common sense or logic behind it is not that important. A week ago I was listening to a station, probably a local one that plays the same song two hundred times, and the person on the station was reporting on gossip news. Stuff about all those celebrities and actors I love so much. But the woman reporting the news, if you want to call it that, made no sense in her report. In one update she mentioned a celebrity taking down a photo online because people didn't like it. Then right after, and I mean mere seconds, the woman joked about a guy who is popular for posting photos that are the same as the celebrity's. One got backlash, the other didn't. Our society makes no sense. People get ridiculed and rewarded for the same thing. I also didn't turn on the TV as I ate because I can't stand commercials. That's not to say that radio doesn't have commercials. They just don't annoy me as much. Probably because I'm out of it half the time it's on. Yesterday I sat for five minutes watching TV commercials. It seemed like an hour. I watched car commercials, of all things. The whole situation just makes me laugh. First off, I know little to nothing about cars. And second, as I watched the commercial I was sitting relaxed in my chair, and yet I was being sold a product that would have me get up off my chair. I'm clearly in no situation to buy a car since I am nowhere near a car, but yet I am still being sold it.

There are always people ready to tell you what's wrong with the world. They aren't all green, but they might as well be. Oh yeah, we aren't very good at solving problems but you can bet your ass we are great at spotting them. You can't go a day without hearing of a tragedy. And we always act like we're surprised. Like it hasn't happened before. What, do we all work at CVS? There will always be another tragic death, another crazy dictator, another radio host who talks in circles. Sometimes I don't want to hear about mutilation or extinction. It doesn't affect me personally. What we are told is relevant and important in our lives may not be so at all.

As soon as the toast was ready, I put on some coffee. We can't use both outlets at the same time or the power will go. The coffee I have is half French vanilla creamer. I don't even know if it is still coffee at that point.

Having coffee in the morning is like cursing to me. I'm pretty sure I'll have an aneurysm if I neglect them. I may just collapse and be rushed to the hospital if I go clean for a little while. The doctor will look at me and ask, "My god. What happened to this man?" And all anyone will say is, "Curses and coffee. The man just couldn't go a day without them."

Despite the greatness of my cooking and that the toast was extremely tasty, easily the most delicious food I will have all day, I ate only a few quick bites before grabbing my backpack and leaving for school.

How much of a writer am I? I carry around a pen and paper wherever I go, even when I have nothing to write. I have to be ready in case I think of some great poetic line or a really clever title for a book. I don't know where inspiration may come along. It's pretty funny that all writers have this delusional idea about their own creativity. We are all just that gifted.

My blue backpack isn't really filled with as many books as you would think. Just a book on Buddhism, my philosophy book I have yet to open, some book about women in the sky, and a few other journalism books from the past year. I should probably empty it since I no longer need them. I'm not practicing Buddhism or anything, I just picked it up one day in the station bookstore after a comedy class. For some idiotic reason Buddhism has to at least be examined by all college students for one day. In that time all college students think that it makes complete sense. No material and all that other crap that should enlighten you. It seems like a decent idea at first; for a while you are on your path to nirvana, you understand life, until the monks start begging you for money and you realize that you spent hours of your time just sitting there when you probably should have been studying.

Don't ask me what any of the books in my bag are actually about unless you want a simple answer. You will only get back-cover review from me. Something that sounds like, "It's a good book." I'm the worst at writing about books. Sure I can read it. Or at the very least skim it. But I'm horrible at in depth discussions about what I read. Probably why I hate school assignments so much.

I feel like this is the part of the story where I'd say something really insightful about life. Maybe some philosophical crap you would learn in class. Or maybe a sociological theory that goes with the theme here. But I have nothing, so I'll just tell you I got in my car. Let's go with the iceberg on this one.

The drive to school is about thirty to forty-five minutes, mostly on the highway. I'm not going to tell you every freaking detail as if I was James Joyce. The cracks in the road are from all the fracking going on around these parts. I'll describe in-depth about the sidewalk and the stone and each bug that I passes as I go down the street. Yeah, not doing that. My drive to school is probably the most boring part of my day. And that's saying something. Nothing exciting happens when I'm driving, because you know, I'm driving.

For some reason, my car is the cleanest thing in my life. Whenever someone goes in it, that's the first thing they say. I, on the other hand, don't view my car as being clean. It's empty. Nothing in the back seats, or the trunk or the passenger seat. It's not that I clean it; I don't put anything in my car to begin with.

I only turn the radio volume to certain numbers when listening to it: two, four, five, six, eight, or ten. Never one, three, seven or nine. I don't really know why I do that. It's not like I will enjoy the song more on volume eight than on volume seven. I make a point to though. I don't go higher than ten or my eardrums will burst. Having told you all that, I didn't put on the radio.

I pulled the car out of the driveway and before I even got off my own block a car cut me off and almost killed me. I responded with a quick, "Jesus Christ," and didn't die.

The most I ever say the words "Jesus Christ" is when I'm driving. If they anointed saints based on that, then I would have been one a long time ago. Every other word out of my mouth is the famous carpenter. Besides that yelling, I had one time I was on the highway and a car nearly hit me again, and instead of just saying, "Jesus Christ!" I didn't hesitate to criticize the other car as the driver continued to drive as if nothing happened. "I hope you get into a fucking car accident where your arms get cut off and before you bleed to death, I hope the car blows up and you become nothing but fucking ashes." That may have been a little much, I admit. Normally I am a very calm driver. I never panic when the gas meter is near empty. If that doesn't show stability in a driver, then I don't know what does.

After I almost got killed, I drove by a lawn crew working on one of the neighbor's lawns. There's usually a group of Latino men working on someone's lawn around here. It's a pain in the ass to get around the truck since it takes up half the street. I have to make sure no car is coming the other direction when that little truck is in the road and it becomes one lane as the guys are working on the grass. There is always one worker who is so close to the curb that I feel like I may hit him. Why do I say it's always Latino men doing that work? Well, because it is. The owners of the lawn company hire them since they work for the least amount of money. Some of the transaction is probably off the books. It helps the owner that the men don't speak much English, since it's tough to negotiate in English when you don't speak it.

I drove by the workers onto the main road around here, Steed Ave. It connects everything: the school, the train station, the town. It's like the *Randall's* of this place.

On the opposite side of the road was an older woman in pink pajamas kneeling over to pick up a cardboard box in the street. Not the safest thing to do. Seniors are always doing unnecessarily dangerous acts that they wouldn't have dared to do if they were younger. I'm not going into the middle of a busy road to pick up a piece of cardboard. But when I'm sixty, I may just walk around town doing it. Who knows?

After stopping at a few red lights and still not getting killed, I cut through the CVS parking lot. I suggest you never go inside that CVS, unless you don't mind waiting forever to buy some soda and chips.

They always act surprised that they have customers. As if they forgot they are open 24/7. Whenever I go inside, there is always a line because they only have one cashier working, until that person decides to call the other worker up to the front. Did you think that the one working away from the cashier was really working? They weren't. They were just wandering the aisles. CVS; it should stand for...well I don't have a joke for it, but their service still sucks.

A group of about ten protesters were outside a store next to the CVS, yelling and proclaiming something I couldn't understand. By the entrance of the store, the protesters had tied down an inflatable rat. You know, to imply the owners are rats. That's the most clever protesters can get, I guess. Unless that rat and chanting is supposed to celebrate the lives of rats. Maybe they are trying to save an endangered rat species.

A cyclist passed by the stores as I cut through. Too bad I didn't hit him. Cyclists are the most obnoxious people ever, wearing their highlighted tight suits and pedaling in the road, as if they are as fast as the cars. Because they are just so athletic, I have to wait for them when I'm driving. Do they know that I'm the one in the car? I can kill them. Just one time I want to drive real close to a cyclist just to scare them. Let them know that the road is not theirs. The only thing that I am thankful for is that it was not a group of cyclists. Oh my god! The whole group of them, all in their gay outfits, acting so important. They clog up half the road, and they're not moving for your car. They become their own mobile traffic stop, slowing down every car behind them.

And no, I didn't go by Stage Five Studios on my way to school. That's in the other direction. I would have had to turn left at the light after the CVS parking lot. I made a right. What is Stage Five Studios? There's a movie studio right down the block from where I live. Some sort of Hollywood around here. If I was smart I'd find a way to be successful over there by the studio while staying around close to home, but I'm not that innovative. I may be going out on a limb here, but I think there are five stages at the studio. Like I said, witty references mean everything.

I was about to get onto the highway, which is a large part of my drive to school, when I got stuck at a red light. And not just any red light. This is the longest red light in town. Five minutes. It takes five minutes for the light to turn green. As I sat there in my car, I stared at the red light and thought that this red light may have cameras on it. But I stopped that thought process pretty quickly.

I try not to think too much about how I have no privacy. That isn't the type of thought that will brighten my day. A good cup of coffee or a good park can do that. I try to ignore how everywhere I go is recorded and I'm being watched. The café, the classroom, the roads: this whole story is on multiple cameras that I don't own and never saw. If there is no camera monitoring me, then someone has a camera ready to record me and my ugly mug. Apparently everyone is an undercover investigative journalist today, ready to tape someone doing something illegal. It makes no sense why someone would want to spy on me, since I'm pretty boring. If you haven't already caught on to that. If someone wanted to they could hack my phone, find all the games I play, all the dirty pictures I store, and all the other crap I have on it. The whole thing terrifies me. We live in fear. But we don't view it that way. We see it as protection. Like the police officers in Penn Station who carry around AK-47's. That's what I want to see when I get off the train and go to the bathroom; a guy with a gun that could kill me several times over. That doesn't make me feel safe. That makes me feel...I don't know. If I wasn't so much of a wiseass, it would terrify you too.

At least I was by a light that had a "no right on red" sign, so there was a reason for me to sit still. Sometimes I'll be in a right lane where you can turn right on red and the one car in front of me won't turn right. Why get into the right lane if you aren't going to turn right on red? People are the worst drivers ever; what makes driving even worse is that they are the only drivers. Want to see a comedy? Drive around here for a few minutes and you'll get some laughs at how people drive.

In the lane next to me was a motorcyclist, who was actually driving correctly. Some of them take advantage of the vehicle's size and squeeze their way through traffic, which irritates me as much as it does any driver. But this guy didn't. And before you ask if he was a middle-aged man going through a midlife crisis, no, the guy was a little older than me.

The motorcyclist was much better to have next to me than the driver who blasts their music for everyone to hear. I didn't get in my car just to listen to your music. I bet he's the guy who sings acapella in the café at school. Do you mind turning that down a little? Or maybe shutting your windows? And it's always the worst song ever. A song that me, or you, or anyone besides this one car would never want to blast from their speakers, and this asshole is in the lane next to you. Oh boy. The best I can hope for is that the car either turns down another road or speeds ahead of me. I don't try to outplay the music in the other car, because it is not worth the effort.

I got on the highway after that short wait.

The school is right off the highway, so once I was done with that riveting thirty-minute part of the drive I was practically there. I only got stopped at one other red light before I could get to hell—I mean, school.

My whole day can be great if I don't hit any lights. If all I hit are green lights for some reason, I'll be in a better mood. Today was not one of those days. I hit every light. Of course as I pulled down the road to the school a car beeped at me. Why? I don't know. People are morons and have no patience.

Where the hell are you going that is so important, anyway? The grocery store? The movies? The doctors? Where the hell are you going that you have to run a red light almost killing me. Please. Please tell me. Because I would love to go to that special, wondrous place.

Part 3 – School

I parked my car in Parking Lot 8, the last resort for anyone parking on campus. If you park there, you're going to walk far to get to your class. It's as if the dean didn't realize the lot was so far off campus until after they made it. You will be so far off campus that you won't actually think you're on campus.

I'm crazy over-parking my car. Sure, it's a piece of shit. Sure, it's old. Sure, it may be the death of me. But I will definitely get it parked between the lines. I'm pretty sure the key to eternal happiness is being able to park your car properly. That and some Buddhist stuff. For me, parking the car is somewhere in the middle of accepting Jesus Christ and listening to Buddha.

Schools are a great place to go if you want to read a bunch of bullshit signs that are supposed to inspire you. Like, *"it's not the end, but the journey that matters"* or *"real victory is from within."* If reading a sign as you walk past inspires you, then you're an idiot. That's the same person who will stop to see the billboards in the city, or will gladly watch hours of dumb television shows. You're really shallow if you let one little line change your outlook on life. I hate school because the first lesson you are taught is that all the good people in the world didn't even need school to change the world. And that they all died horrific deaths. Jesus, Gandhi, Socrates; none of them went to school, and when they changed the world they got killed for it. What a lesson.

What's even better than that is when you learn about the life of great writers like Dickens and Shakespeare. Schools always try to present them as upper class individuals who had years of formal schooling and they gloss over their actual lives. You probably have more of a formal education than they ever had if you're reading them. Yes, they were smart, but let's not act like they spent all their time in a classroom. Think about it; we are teaching work by men who lacked formal education as a part of our formal education. It's pretty funny.

If lessons aren't your thing then you can always find a sign on the wall for a club or event in the school. Every club has an event, every event has a sign, and every wall is filled with those signs, and because every club needs to make their sign special, every sign has different colors, fonts, pictures, sizes, paper, and just about anything else you can think of to get your attention. Because God forbid someone doesn't read your sign about a Bible study or newspaper club. You can't walk down a hallway without reading some bullshit promotion. I'm pretty sure I read a book-worth of signs by now.

I was late to class. If you're surprised by that, you must have just woken up or are reading the wrong book. The door was closed since the class already began. The classroom is really wide so that means there is plenty of room for seats and enthusiastic students. About thirty to forty of us can fit in the four long rows. I don't like going over people when I'm late. It makes me feel like I'm getting in their way or distracting them, which I am, since I have to become like a contortionist just to squeeze by. Sometimes people will give you that look, you know it, as if they can't believe that you're late. Like I'm breaking some law by arriving at such a time. Meanwhile that person probably never studies and sells something on the side. I picked the closest seat available to me as I entered, next to some tall bearded guy who was falling out of his desk that, unlike the rest of the room, was perpendicular to the teacher. It's not that the desk was broken or anything. He just may have been hungover. He was too big for the seat, so big that his feet could touch the first row of seats. He had on a dark blue t-shirt with a green baggy jacket and khaki shorts that didn't fit. He really was paying attention to the teacher alright, playing whatever mobile game he had on his phone while listening to whatever type of music blasted through his headphones. Probably playing the same song over and over again, convinced that the songwriter wrote the stupid lyrics for him. At least he had his headphones on both ears. That's being honest to the teacher since you won't even listen to anything they say. Some students have an earpiece in only one ear as they pretend to pay attention. Come on, we know you don't want to be there. The one ear thing won't fool anyone. That student must think he is real clever for doing that. He's the type of guy who would think for hours about a witty nickname for someone and when he tells you about it, he'll act all smart, like he is the only guy who has ever thought of anything smart in his life.

I don't apologize to the teacher when I'm late. That means I feel bad for wasting the teacher's time, which I don't. I have a life too. Teachers today think what they're doing is so damn difficult; meanwhile, all they're doing is reading out of a freaking textbook. All of them just assume they are teaching the most important subject ever and the worst part is they think you care.

I can't tell sometimes if the teachers are here for me or for themselves. I mean, who grows up wanting to be a professor? No one. No one grows up wanting to teach Einstein and Shakespeare. No. You want to be them. Until you get to be like a hopeless music student and come to realize that the best you can be is a teacher of what you love. You can't be a composer so you are just a professor of it instead. Some professors don't care about their students. Only about advancing their own careers. Yeah, right now you're teaching me but as soon as you write a bestseller or Hollywood calls about that screenplay you wrote, you'll leave this campus. You won't even think about how you once taught this class. In your bio, that part of your life will be mentioned as if it was a waste of time. *"Before her bestseller, she taught at (some college I never heard of)."* Professors are just pissed off failures in whatever field they are in. And they are the ones I want telling others about my work. Great.

I had a professor—I don't remember her name— in my freshman year that only taught the class so she could learn the material. Every class she'd bring up a children's book she was writing even though it was a new media class, which is supposed to be about all the new forms of mass communication. Not a children's book. She'd even ask the tech nerd in the class questions for how to use new media to promote her book. What was the book about? I don't know. It had to do something with teaching kids how to learn while having fun. So it was like every kid's book.

The communications building where I had my newspaper writing class—and I'm not making this up— has a Wall of Fame for all of the accomplishments of great alumni and professors. And guess who is on the wall? The same professor from last semester with her children's book. That goes to show you that teaching didn't mean as much to her as she tried to make you think. The school asked her for an accomplishment in her life and teaching was not her answer.

My current philosophy professor, Mr. Wenington, has been lecturing before I was born. He may have helped build the school. You could tell he was out of touch with the youth, which by that, I mean me. He didn't get us, how we were, or what we liked. He'd read this and in a very sophisticated manner criticize the structure and format of this book and claim it to be the end of literature as we know it. He wanted what was best for us, but he didn't know how to communicate with us. He came from the ideology that said students should be pushed to learn and that hard work is to be expected from them. Not good grades. He gave us a lot to read each class thinking we were brought up like him. I believe I read one of those assignments. It may be somewhere in my room.

Luckily for me, I didn't miss anything. I mean, in the class lesson. Not the previous assignments.

"I'd like to pose a question to you which is on the board." He pointed to the white board that had his question written in black marker. It struck me that I never realize how much I hate school until I'm actually in school. Until I'm sitting in my desk and the teacher has begun talking and the lesson has started. Damn. Nothing like a late epiphany. I'm no better than that dumb zombie kid.

"What is your obligation to humanity?" He turned back to face the class and continued talking to no one.

"Does being a human obligate you to commit acts to maintain society as it is? Should you be generous to a stranger? Say "thank you"? Or can you disagree with all that we define as humane? Could you do none of the sort and let a world of chaos and anarchy run wild? Would you be wrong to not care for the…"

He stopped for a second and noticed for the first time that no one was listening. He must have thought an example would grab our attention. It didn't.

"The post-apocalyptic world seems to be very popular among the youth today. So let's say this: What if the apocalypse happens? That show you watch where the characters live in a post-apocalyptic world, that's real. Now whether you see that as merely art or a dark prediction of mankind's future, should you care about it, if it were to happen? For real, in this instance." He leaned his back against the table in front of the board. "Let's say that is our eventual outcome. That by the end of this year the human race will be no more." He pointed at us as he emphasized our not being here. But at that point we already were. "You. Me. All you know, gone. Should you do what you can to save us or just live your life? "

Still no one raised their hands. Since the example prolonged the silence instead of sparking conversation, he tried to speak like one of us. "In layman terms, what I'm asking you is does the mere fact that you are a human require you to live a certain lifestyle?"

No hands.

He reasoned with himself. "I gave you no homework with the hope that we could discuss this topic." As if I would've done the reading if he'd assigned it. When I learned we had no homework, I didn't even think about the possibility of a class discussion. I just thought it was great to have no homework. See what I mean when I say out of touch?

He thinks we're all going home religiously reading the textbook each and every night. We're not. We're just hoping for no homework and no final. And if there is a final, that it has a bell curve.

Still nothing.

"Does anyone have anything to say about this? Do any of you have an opinion on your own demise? Because I am not going to stand up here all class and listen to myself talk."

Coming to the realization that we were fine with not participating, he put his papers into his suitcase and folded it. "Well your silence is deafening." He didn't officially end class, but we all got the hint. "I hope this great class discussion didn't make you forget the time of our next class." And he left.

The twenty or so of us just sat there for five minutes confused at what just happened. At least it felt like five minutes. It may have been shorter.

The guy next to me finally removed his headphones. "What'd he say?"

A brunette girl who was sitting in the large front rows of tables facing the teacher got up first. "Class is over."

He jumped up. "Awesome." I guess his hangover wore off.

I grabbed my backpack and followed the line of students leaving the class.

Believe it or not, he was actually much better than the philosophy professor I had last semester, and not just because he let us leave early with no homework. She was an Asian woman who was just a rude, mean bitch, and actually told the class that if she saw some of us outside of school, she wouldn't be so nice to us. I can't help but feel she may have been talking about me there. Who says that? That's someone who's responsible for the education of the youth of this country. Yeah. I am as sad to hear that as you are. It probably didn't help that I wrote my final about philosophy being pointless. Looking back on it, that wasn't the best decision I've made academically. That and joining the newspaper club were two bad moves. Aside from actually going to school, but that one is kind of obvious. Anyway, I thought I had a good case, or at least had some reasoning behind it. My argument was that every philosophy is more worried about getting you to agree with them than anything else. The philosophers say they want truth. But I said that's bullshit. Don't worry, I didn't curse in my paper. I'm not that much of an idiot. The philosophers want their truth to be right. It isn't truth if they don't agree with it. They want people to listen to them and their take on truth and the world, which let's face it, we all do. It isn't about the actual people learning the truth or of the world, but the philosophers being right. Although the philosophers would never say that. I then went on to say that it's you who can find truth in your life. You don't need a philosopher to tell you what's wrong or what's right, or how to live, or anything like that. You must learn it for yourself. Develop your own philosophy. Philosophers have too much of an agenda to only rely on them. If it weren't for my study habits, the paper would have been great. It wasn't. I got a D on it. I bet she gave me a bad grade because she thought I was a good student when she met me. See, for the first few weeks of school or so, I am a good student. I raise my hand. I answer questions. I participate and show interest in the class. Then I stop. I get tired of being told what to do and what to think about something and I barely pass.

Think that's bad? Wait till I tell you about my sociology class.

I took the enlightening class last semester and, well, it didn't go too well. We had to write a response to a video the professor showed in class. What was the video about? You are asking the wrong person if you want to know, because I apparently wrote the improper reaction. When I got the paper back, all I saw across the top written in red ink was, *"You should watch the film again."*

What does that mean? Did I not get the point she was trying to teach? How the hell can my interpretation of a film be wrong? It is sociology for God's sake! The whole study is based on interpretations! People make up fancy terms and have studies and findings and what do they do with them? Interpret them! How can I be wrong with how I view the film in a field that encourages discovery through investigation? I just didn't understand her comment. I guess she didn't want me to give my opinion. She wanted me to give the opinion she'd like to hear.

Sociology is all messed up. They think we students are so dumb that the only way to teach us of the science is to relate it to modern stuff we like. I hated that I couldn't just read the textbook for the information, when I did read the textbook, that is. No, the book related studies to television shows and movies and celebrity news that I have to know also. Of course, the book stated it's what young people wanted so they included the information. Obviously they didn't ask me because I would have said no. Why do I need to know of entertainment in order to learn sociology? Who came up with that? Is that how much we care about it? The only way for me to understand the world is to know the bullshit entertainment industry first? You know, the one where every scene is setup and the jackasses are all fake. That's the world I'm using to make conclusions about the real world. And guess what the name of the book was? *The Real World*. Right there they are trying to present the fakeness as real. Fuck the world with the bullshit they call lessons. If that is how they are teaching then I'll gladly misinterpret every video they show me. They don't care if I learn the information for myself, they only want me to learn the information the way they want me to see it. People are always trying to tell you their way to view the world, from radio hosts, to philosophers, to professors. It's all rhetoric. Though it is odd for me to even mention this since I'm telling you how people are telling you how to view the world in their way. Figure that one out.

On my way downstairs I saw a sign for a writing meeting later today. It was about some writing program having a meeting in the science building. Of all the signs on the wall it was the most bland. Just black and white lettering stating the time and place. It mentioned how there would be refreshments and had pictures related to writing around the border, like pens and notebooks. I could already tell that I would have some great conversation with the interesting person who made this awesome sign.

Despite the plain appearance, I ripped the white piece of paper off the wall and took it for myself.

As I left the building, I held a door open for a girl walking out, because you know, I'm that kind of guy. After she exited, one person went by, two people, three people...eight people walked by without even saying thank you. I didn't know the parade was in town. How many people can walk through an open doorway without saying thanks before you shut the door on them? My limit is five. I would have let go sooner but the people were walking close to each other. It took me a few seconds to let go of the door as I was still surprised at the ignorance of the walkers.

By the time the ninth rude idiot got to the door, I gave up. I'm not a goddamn doorman. I let go of the door. It may have hit the person. Maybe not. I can't tell you because I walked away before it slammed shut. What can I say? I may be the nicest asshole you've ever met.

After that I sat down on a bench outside to work on my jokes. I got nothing done because they needed a lot of editing and I'm too lazy to be precise with my words. Another student was kneeling by some rocks a few feet away from me, a white baseball cap with the words *"John Cage"* spray-painted in black sat crooked on his head. His shirt had more colors and shades than any other shirt I've ever seen and his jeans were too tight. I could tell he was an art major because he had an openness about life that others don't have. He had to; no normal human can sit next to rocks and be intrigued.

Art majors live a real happy life, where they sing hello to everyone, ask them how they are doing, and strike up a conversation to fill the silence. It's not normal. Most people can sit quiet for a few minutes. They can take out their phone and read updates. Text a friend they will see later that day. Not art majors though. They live life as if it's a stage. It can really lead to awkward moments.

He gleefully started a conversation you know I wasn't going to. "Hey, how're you doing?"

"Not bad." I wasn't really in the mood to talk. I was more focused on my jokes than anything this guy had to say.

"Do anything interesting today?" See what I mean? I'm telling you art majors are too nice. Their kindness makes me sick. They all act like they have some great insight into the human mind and it gets old quick.

"No." I didn't ask him anything about his day because I didn't want to further the conversation.

Unfortunately, my quiet indifference didn't shut him up. Some people don't understand when their opinion is not wanted.

"I'm working on my next artistic piece." He waited for a response I didn't give. "Still working on the name of it, but it's supposed to represent the betrayal one feels when being in a situation where they do not know the way out. It shows the passion one feels if the world turns their back...."

"It's a rock." His "art" was some rocks lined up in a circle.

"That's what a non-artist would see."

"It's a rock." Idiot.

He was still talking to me, but seemed to be talking as if he was performing. "You don't understand art. How an artist lives. How I live. I don't live like all the other minds of the world. I live by my emotions and feelings, not by numbers and test scores. You have to let an artist be an artist. This piece of depth and emotion is too much for people to fully grasp at first."

"Uh-huh." I wasn't listening. I was staring at my piece of paper trying to work on my jokes. Whenever people talk to me, they don't actually talk to me. It's more or less that I'm the closest person to them when they just so happen to spurt out a thought or two.

He wasn't done talking, as if anyone was listening. "Let the authors write novels. Let the performers take the stage. Let the artists be. We are not robots programmed by numbers. We are humans with a soul and a heart. Let those who want to express their souls express them to the world."

"Yeah. Sure." I had no idea what he was talking about.

"The world is art! You can create anything with an artistic mind."

I had about enough of his rambling. "What about that?" I pointed to the school map five feet across from the bench.

"What?"

"That. The map. Is that art?"

"Yes it is." He answered way too confidently for such a subjective question.

"You can't just go around saying everything is art just because you want it to be."

"Isn't that proving my point?" he slyly answered.

"Whatever."

I'm surprised my tight pants debater didn't have a buddy to back him up since all art majors stick together. They must have a creed or something. Last semester I was in an art class that was supposed to teach me the beauty of art. Right up my alley. It didn't though. I don't know why but I got there early for some reason. The class was full of art, music, and theater majors. You could tell by their flamboyant attitudes. They made sure to tell me they were art, music, and theater majors. I didn't know any of them personally, but I recognized some of them since they were in my class, so I did what any sane student would do in that situation. I sat down in the empty seat at the table. That's another thing too. The classroom had no desks. Just a large brown table. Must be one of those artsy ideas to promote their creativity.

The teacher in the class was a real arrogant guy too. You think that Mr. Wenington would criticize this book? Please, that would be nothing compared to what this guy would do to it. He would not only mock this whole story, he'd write a full blown book on his opinion in another language stating any inaccuracies and complications he had with the manner in which this story was told. All just to prove that he was smarter than me. Like I didn't get it when he told the class about all of his musical accomplishments even though it was an art class and started to speak in German just for the hell of it. After saying a few German words he'd explain what he just said, which included words like hence and therefore, or thereby, or in conclusion, as if he was writing a political document about the rights of man. I'm convinced that the word hence has never been used in a joke, only when smart people are trying to make a point. He thought so much of his intelligence that when I met him he even tried to guess my ethnicity just by looking at my last name. Yeah, definitely not a guy who you want to be around too long.

Pausing from his self-praising, he turned to face me. "Why are you here?"

I was already sitting and didn't know how to answer him. "Do you mean in a philosophical sense or a practical one?"

Turns out there was a double class with the same students and I was one of the few not in both. And no one decided to tell me. I had to wait for the arrogant composer to ask me a vague question. Anyway that's how all art majors are. They all stick together and act like everyone's always watching them or waiting for them to sing. It can really drain on you. I should be happy that John Cage was alone. If he was with someone, I may have had to hear a song and dance.

You ever go somewhere because you hope someone else is there? Not because you really like the place?

That's why I went to the café. Not for the food, or to write jokes. But to see Jacqueline.

She was an aspiring nurse who I met in Early American History last semester. We spoke one afternoon in the café. And we talked. And talked. And talked. About everything. One of those conversations where the content didn't matter as much as the time. She told me how she was going to nursing school after the year and this would be her last semester. I didn't have the courage to ask for her number. I'm a wimp with stuff like that. I probably shouldn't get all worked up about meeting her. It's not like we were friends. Doug and I are more friends. We were classmates who spoke after class. Nothing special. But I still really liked talking to her. I could lay my guard down while we sat together. It's funny how you can talk to some people forever, when you can't even stand the sight of others. Why does it seem that I'm always having conversations with people I hate? Also she had a wit other women just don't have. And she was cute as hell too.

I really think she was a good person with a genuinely good heart and whenever I get down, like when I can't sleep, I think that there are good people out there like her, so all isn't lost. Not everyone is a jerk, or a bastard, or a wiseass. There are some people who are actually helping others. Maybe if I make it as a comedian she'll attend one of my shows and we'll talk after the show about seeing each other again. Or maybe I'll write a best seller and she'll recognize my name on the bookshelf and tell everyone about the writer she used to know. I'd like to be her white knight, her hero, her man. But I'm not. I'm just me. A smartass punk who can't let a simple thing go.

Maybe it's better that I don't ever see her again. I should let her beauty and goodness be my memory of her. If I see her again, I'll learn things about her that will make me change my mind. And knowing me, I'll go the other way after that. I think that's my problem with some of my friends now, like Natacha. I know too much about her. I spent too much time with her after classes ranting about the struggles of school. We are at the point in our relationship where secrets have to be revealed. And I'm not good with crap like that. I don't like people enough to learn of the shit that they have to deal with. When they start telling me their personal problems, I leave.

Every time I go to the café, I hope to see the reddish-brunette sitting alone in the corner reading from a textbook. Sometimes I think it's her, but it never is.

Instead of seeing the girl I dream about, a person drove up to me asking for directions in the café's parking lot.

"Do you know where the Cluster A Building is? "Yeah. It's that way." I pointed where I thought it was

"Thank you." And he drove off.

Ah crap. I just realized that I gave him the wrong directions. That building, I mean Cluster A, is the other way. If he goes the way I pointed, he is going in the complete opposite direction. Well, nothing I could do at that point, he was gone.

I don't know why but some of the buildings in the school are labeled as clusters. Maybe it was some joke played by the dean. He thought everyone would get a good laugh if he told the architects to name the buildings clusters, but he never actually intended on that happening. So now he just plays it cool, like it's no big deal, like he planned it. But it was a mistake all along.

Most at the school will say that the label is to easier identify the buildings for the students. Yeah. And the high school built a football stadium for my education. The school must really think I'm stupid if they don't even think I can get to class without the buildings being explicitly called something other than a building. I want to say that the clusters go up to letter H, but I don't look at the school map often enough to remember. When I do notice it, I am questioning its artistic integrity. What I got from the alphabetized clusters is that one of them is called Cluster F. I consider that a warning by the school to anyone who takes classes there. It is kind of them to tell me where the Clusterfuck is. Although that could be the name of the school and I'm not sure I'd know the difference.

I then bumped into someone in the plaza that I wasn't expecting to see for at least another week: my newspaper editor. I'm apart of the school newspaper. Please hold back the applause. I try not to tell anyone because nothing good has ever come from it.

"How is the article coming along?"

"Great. I'm just about done with it." I haven't started it.

Damian went on to talk about when the article was due and other newspaper club stuff that you wouldn't find interesting. Hell, I don't even find half of what he says about the club interesting, and I'm in the club. He was much more excited about the publication of the newspaper than I was. I could care less if the damn thing ever sees the light of day. As for him, you can tell that all he did was think about getting the newspaper completed. I bet that's why he has such a long beard. Poor guy is so stressed out over the newspaper club that he forgot about shaving. Our conversation ended shortly after his updates. We had nothing to talk about besides the club so we said goodbye to one another before the exchange got awkward.

A few weeks ago I was assigned to write an article about Midnight Madness, which is when all the sports teams introduce themselves to whoever is crowded in the gym. Each athlete gets their name called. There are dances done by five different dance groups the school has and they run silly contests. Like someone would shoot a basketball from half court. Stuff like that. Somehow the gym was full of people for the can't-miss event. I just stood there by the indoor track above the gym looking down on the spectacle. The atmosphere was too boring for me to sit down and enjoy the night. It's almost like the school thought, *"How can we come up with an event that will show the false enthusiasm our students have for being here?"* The whole thing is just sports propaganda with pompoms. Ironically enough, I am the one writing the story promoting the night. No one likes going to school that much. I don't care who you are. And don't tell me about school spirit. What school spirit? Our school sucks at basically every sport. I shouldn't have lied to Damian about my article. He will be very upset when he learns I didn't complete it.

We live in a time where you get information instantly on your phone and what is this poor guy doing to advance his career? Running a print newspaper that will be outdated as soon as it hits the stands. Nobody cares for it anyway. This campus doesn't have that much going on that people need to read the newspaper. What are they going to read? About a wall in the communications building? Or a professor writing a children's book? That's first class journalism.

An environmentalist came up to me before I could enter the café. You know the type. They feel the world is going to burn tomorrow and the end is upon us. They wear their white t-shirts with an innocent animal in the center of it and hand out multi-colored recycled pamphlets with a bunch of facts to support their claim.

What annoys me the most is their subtle arrogance in the way they talk. Like they are better than me because they care about a polar bear or because they recycle.

The green guy reached out to give me a pamphlet, which I rejected. "Save the planet. By 2040 the artic ice will be completely gone." Gotta have those reliable facts.

Now I could have said some wiseass remark like, *"Oh too bad. There goes my vacation plans."* Or, *"That stinks. My drinks will have no ice in them."* I didn't though. I tried to be polite and make a nice face and just walk by. It didn't work. The green guy jumped in front of me as if he was Carl from my comedy class. The difference here is that Carl was much fatter and this guy was yelling at me instead of into a microphone. "Don't you care about the polar bears?" Like all I do is go around pondering about the polar bears, wondering if they are alright. Let me tell you this, I care about the polar bears as much as they care about me.

I looked at him in disgust for a second before stepping around him. That's the type of question that irritates me. They want me to feel bad about their concerns. It's not bad enough that the world is going to hell. No, these green people have to rub it in my face that I'm apart of the problem. We have to get it in our heads that we are at the mercy of Mother Nature, not the other way around. If the ice caps are going to melt, then they are going to melt. What the hell am I supposed to do all the way from the café at a local college? Oh, let me stop smoking this one cigarette. I'll just throw out this one plastic bottle. I'm sure that will stop the millions of pounds of ice from melting.

I didn't walk inside the main cafeteria because it's always too crowded. Too many people for my taste, and too noisy. There is barely any room to move around since every table is packed. For our enjoyment the music majors sometimes sing for the hell of it for everyone to hear. In the middle of lunch, four or five of them will start an acapella song as if anyone wants to hear that crap. And everyone in the place loves it and applauses afterwards. I don't. I don't go to the café to see a show. I go to eat and meet some friends. Don't act like you're doing me a favor by singing during my lunch. You're not. Oh and the food. Oh my god. The food. It is disgusting. Name a food that they serve and it's gross enough to make you run to the bathroom shortly after eating it. The best tasting meal is a bag of chips and those have maybe five chips since half of it is air. Stay away from anything in the café. You will regret it. Avoid it, even if the school does give you a gift card for twenty-five dollars worth of food. Or at least, what they call food. Instead of dealing with cold pizza as the tenors sing a tune, I went to the downstairs café that is much smaller and only filled during lunch.

That's when I saw the girl of my dreams sitting by the corner table. Yeah. I'm just messing with you. That didn't happen. I told you this wasn't a romance.

There was a woman, about sixty or so, standing by a small table on the wall opposite from the rest of the room. She wore a purple dress and had the look of someone who needed a beer and was already tired with the day. As she packed up the table, I walked over to her.

"Are you doing tarot readings?"

"Yeah. I'm about done. But I got time for one more." I took a seat in the red folding chair and she stopped packing her supplies and sat down in hers. I thought she was going to get all deep with some psychic view of the world, maybe tell me the future right away. She didn't though. She just reported on her day. "Today was a slow day. Tomorrow will be better. I'll be upstairs."

"Yeah," I answered. "There are more people upstairs." I only agreed because I had nothing to really say. Sometimes I do that and look pretty dumb.

I picked out three cards from the pack as she instructed me to. Yeah, I don't know the least about tarots or their meanings, or why I even sat down. I honestly thought people were pronouncing the word carrot wrong when I heard it. I'd describe the cards to you but I had no idea what I was looking at. Each card represents something though, which is where the tarot reader comes in. The cards did look like they belonged on a book cover, imaginative with their colorful designs.

She did her best to explain the cards to me. "This one is your past, your present and your future. Give me your palms." I don't know why she needed my palms, but I went with it anyway.

She read the cards. I mean, I think that's what she was doing. "You have a strong subconscious and you give off a lot of energy." A lot of energy? Is that why I'm always tired? Someone once said to me that I have an old soul. I don't know what that means. According to that theory, this story is written by someone who died a few centuries ago. That can't be worse than that brain in a vat theory.

"That's good right?" I didn't know what to make of her comments. I chose to be quiet and let her do her thing. Must have been all of my energy. Seriously though, there is a strange feeling I got when I was sitting there. It could have been my energy. Or maybe the effects of the coffee were wearing off.

"Your past...it is apart of you. It is you. This past has shaped your identity. Have you lost a family member recently?"

"No." That threw her off.

"Oh. Well, your past suggests otherwise. As if you are one with this unwanted burden of loss." She lost me.

"Your present. I see you are on a journey. This empty road is ahead of you. You are just beginning this journey and have to decide for yourself where this road takes you. Have you started any new endeavors lately?"

I thought about it for a second. "Hmm. Nothing that I could think of. Well, I guess school."

"This school is your road. And you will travel down the road it has for you."

"Okay." I was still confused.

"Your future holds much promise. I see many successes in your life. You are the king of wherever you go."

"Well that's good." I'm such a king that I don't even view myself as one. "What should I do to become this king?"

"Let me see." She took a second and examined the cards. "I have two pieces of advice for you. Beware what lies on the empty road, for it is easy to get lost on a road with no signs."

"What's the other?"

"Know that some darkness hides in the light."

"Okay." I was really out of words to say at that point. But to be fair, she lost me as soon as she started talking.

After that exchange she packed up her stuff and wished me well. So according to a possibly drunk carrot reader, I will be king one day. Sounds like she was messing with me when I say it like that.

I took a seat at an empty tan table. At least I tried to. I put my backpack on the table for four, but when I tried to sit down, I fell out of the chair. It was broken. Nobody flinched at my spill. I got up and took notice of all the people who seemingly didn't catch my slip.

Four future teachers were discussing their boyfriend problems. About how Jimmy did this and won't do that. And how George just doesn't talk enough. Clearly stuff I'm interested in. Three friends are making inside jokes I'm on the outside of. You'd have thought they were all comedians, the way they're laughing. They had two tables with four chairs each. Why the hell do three people need eight chairs to sit in? That's just inconsiderate. Everyone else in the small café is concentrating so much, I swear you'd think they were curing cancer, but really they're studying a subject like philosophy. You can go real far with a degree in that. You ever notice how the smartest people never have to study the hardest? Yet the hardest workers are never the best students? There was a girl at one table who, like me, was sitting alone, but unlike me was actually studying. You could tell the effort was getting to her. She was too focused. Too concentrated on what she was doing. Some would say that type of person is a hard worker who gets the most out of their abilities. I call them dumb. Because a smart person wouldn't have to work so hard, because they are smart enough to know that if they do work too hard, they will have no energy afterwards.

I actually did recall seeing the three comedians in the café before. They were music majors or actors. Maybe both. They definitely spoke as if they were giving a performance and they were ready to sing at any given moment. I shouldn't speak too soon, because they just may do it.

You know, I always wanted to be in a band just so I could quit. I wouldn't be in one for the fame or the girls. No. I would love to just walk into the studio one day and curse out my band mates. "Screw you guys. I do all of the work. I'm out of here." I'd slam my guitar emphatically just to make my exit even more awesome. Too bad I suck at that sort of stuff. You know being a musician. Or I'd totally do it.

I must have fallen asleep shortly after that because the next thing I remember is Moose waking me up.

Moose is a nice guy, for the most part. By that I mean he will never be on the news for killing someone or whatever. If he ever did something bad, it would only be because he wanted to fit in, not because he's really a bad guy. That's Moose's problem; he cares so much about what people think of him that he'd be okay with jeopardizing his integrity for popularity.

He isn't really my friend. I know that "friend" has taken on a new meaning over the past few years because of social media, but I'm talking about the old definition of a friend: a person that you can rely on. I'll never call him up to hang out or get invited to his birthday party (that is, if I knew when it was). But if he sees me sleeping in the café alone, he'll walk over and start a conversation. That's the type of friend he is, an acquaintance.

He isn't very patient. Moose never sits still because he's always worried that he's missing out on what society tells him is important. *"What's next?"* is practically his life motto. This guy never lives a day at a time. He isn't even here right now. I can't say for certain if he was looking for me or not. He may have been searching for someone else and just so happened to see me.

"What's up?" He didn't acknowledge that he woke me up. It took me a second to fully wake up.

"Nothing much, you?"

Because he's as alert as am I, Moose sat in the busted chair and nearly fell over. He didn't though. He regrouped himself and sat in the chair across from me. It's not that I wanted him to sit in the bad chair. It just happened so quickly that by the time I reacted, he was already falling over. I shouldn't say I reacted. I didn't. I more or less watched him nearly hurt himself due to the great furniture at this school.

"I just got back from my Political Theory class. The teacher's an asshole. He won't even give the class a bell curve on the last test so we're all going to fail." For those of you who don't know, a bell curve is a clever trick that teachers can use to help the stupid or lazy students pass the class. Instead of giving out regular grades, the teacher gives them out according to their relation with other students. The student with the highest grade, even if it is low, like a 65 or whatever, would get an A and the lowest grade of the class would get a F. Students love this method because it helps out all those who did awful on a test and just wanted a B.

You wouldn't know Moose came from a class by looking at him. He had no books with him, not even a backpack, just his football jersey with his name on it.

"That sucks." I was always confused with bell curves in schools. I could never tell if they meant that the teachers were too tough or the students were too dumb.

Moose complained about his academic performance. I know from experience it's easier to bitch about failing than actually passing. "Schools are so stupid with their grades and everything." Said the man who's barely passing.

"Maybe we're the idiots." I really didn't want to hear a moron make a fuss about failing on intelligence-based tests. "What I mean is, if we're sitting here complaining about how bad it is, then why are we here?" Moose didn't say anything. If you say something with just a little bit of thought, you lose him.

Here he is spending so much time bitching about school, yet he still spends the money to go to classes. He hasn't stopped going, despite his frustration with the system. Maybe the school isn't the one with the problem. I don't know. Sometimes I think it's me. Other times I can't really tell. But when I think it's me, I'm really convinced it's me to the point that it's weird. Honestly, I can't tell half the time if I'm the weirdo, or if everyone else is.

He ignored my comment and continued to talk about his class, which I didn't have much interest in. What? I said I was an acquaintance, not a friend. "Well at least the speaker didn't show." I said nothing. "We were supposed to have some expert give the class a speech on some new political theory, but the guy never showed up so the professor let us go early."

"Oh. That's nice." I changed topics. "What's with the shirt?" Moose was wearing a red football jersey with the number 74 in green letters and his nickname on the back.

Some college students are always wearing jerseys or uniforms to represent whatever frat or club they're in. You can't go to a campus without seeing a student in a uniform. Campuses that promote themselves as liberation centers for a student's life, a platform to better help a student discover their calling, somehow manage to all look the same.

"I'm going to the city tonight to join a fraternity. This is the last test we have to do before joining. They gave me this jersey as preparation for tonight."

"What exactly do you have to do?"

"I don't know. They said they would tell us when we were there. Hey…" He stopped for a second. "Why don't you come along? Maybe they'll let you in the frat."

"No." You couldn't pay me to be in a fraternity.

"Oh, come on."

"No. I'm not going to pay for friends." That last remark hurt Moose a little bit. It was too honest for him, because he knows as well as I do that the guys in the frat don't like you for who you are, but for being one of them. I'm more of a friend to this guy, since I don't require him to pass a test to talk to me.

"You know what time it is?"

"No." He made no attempt to check his phone. I should have known that he wouldn't know the time.

He doesn't even bring books around with him, why would he be aware of the time? "You have another class?" he asked me.

"Yeah. I should probably get going. Don't want to be late. At least not too late."

"Ok. I'm done for the day." He enjoyed telling me that, as if it was some great accomplishment on his part. Like he got away with something by having the rest of the day off.

I picked up my backpack from the table and stood up. "I gotta go. I'll see you around."

"I got the same class same time next week. I'll see you here then."

"Ok." I tried to make up for that low blow I said earlier. "Good luck with your frat friend thing, get-together, party, whatever you call it. Good luck."

"Thanks." He appreciated my way of apologizing. I'm the worst at saying sorry. Must be an ego thing. I don't think I've ever said the words "I'm sorry" ever in my life. I apologize, but if the person doesn't know me and doesn't realize that I'm apologizing, they think I'm an asshole.

Still needing the time, I walked over to someone reading in the corner of the café on my way out.

"Hey." I tried to get his attention. "Do you know what time it is?"

He put his book down and yelled, "Fuck off, I'm reading!" I looked over at Moose who was too busy on his phone to notice the confrontation. I mean, what do you say to that? Sorry, I'm sure that book is so good that you can't even give me the fucking time. What an asshole! I left in frustration and still unaware of the time. The world doesn't even make sense anymore. Some people are just assholes. There's no nice way for me to put it.

Before heading back upstairs, I went to the bathroom. If there is one good thing about college, it's the bathrooms. The food may kill you and the professors will fail you, but at least you can go in a clean area with tiny floor tiles and white sinks. There is something ironic about that, but I can't put my finger on it. As I tell you about the cleanliness, there was a guy in the stall next to me doing none other than taking a dump. The whole room smelled. I could barely breath. I did my best to cover my nose with my shirt and go number one in the urinal. I swear there is always someone taking a dump in the stall next to me.

After that experience I headed back over to the science building where my second class was taking place. Before going to the second floor, I went through the downstairs corridor of the building. The corridor is one of the prettiest places on campus with the marble floor and clean white look. The janitors never have to clean this corridor since it's always empty. It's much nicer than either cafés. Yet for some reason no one ever sits there. I have no idea why the cleanest and most comfortable place to be on campus is never occupied by anyone. Just a few pamphlets and cards on the table for upcoming events taking place on campus. I doubt anyone has ever stopped to look at one.

I started sneezing when I got inside; must have been all the dust in the room. When I got to my third sneeze a voice said, "God bless you." The voice didn't wait for me to respond with a witty remark. Too bad. Since I would have said something smart like, *"I hope he did."* My comebacks in my head are always better than anything I actually say.

"You know what the best part of the world is?" the voice said.

"No. What?" I wiped my nose with the inside part of my shirt. I rubbed my eyes with my jacket. The outside of it. I'm not that much of a pig.

"The sky. It has no prejudice. Some parts of nature do. Trees only grow in tree lines. Ice in only 273 Kelvin. But not the sky. Tomorrow when you wake up, you can look up and see it. Say what you want about the sun and moon, but they are only there half the time. The sky comes in all different assortments; rain clouds, gray clouds, no clouds like today, but regardless, it will always be there. I believe the reason the sky is above us is so we always have something to look up to each day of our lives, and that maybe by looking up to it literally, we'll learn to look up figuratively as well. The day that happens, my work will be done."

By the time I was done getting myself together between my sneezes and rubbing my eyes, the voice was gone. I never got a good look at him. I turned to see if anyone was around me in the corridor. I even walked back outside from the way I entered to catch a glimpse of the voice. But no one was there. It was just me.

I continued on my way to my next class after that unique back and forth. Sometimes I really can converse with people. When I got to the room, there was a sign on the door that read, *"Mr. Lester's Beginning Chemistry is canceled for today."* It took me a second to realize that Mr. Lester isn't my teacher and I don't take Beginning Chemistry. Too bad.

The actual teacher of my class is Mrs. Gallo, a pregnant British woman with short curly hair. I don't really have any sarcastic remark about her. She is a really nice lady, probably the nicest person on campus. Plus she's British, so that has to count for something. I wish I had a British accent. It is a proven fact that British people sound smarter than everyone else. I would have been at Randall's by now if I was British. But I'm not, clearly.

I don't like the class because it does nothing for me. I only take it to fulfill the requirements because apparently a guy who is trying to be a journalist needs to learn about science. That's what my Midnight Madness story needs, some equations or experimental studies. I'm too stupid to be a scientist. I don't know about pons or Kelvins and I don't care for any of it. It's so boring. No wonder no one cares about global warming. Have you seen the presentations on it? I'd take making wisecracks about dead writers over learning about the Earth collapsing.

When I entered the room, I sat in the desk by the door. A sign-in sheet was going around for attendance, which I think is a much better way of keeping attendance than calling out every student's name, like some other teachers I have. I signed the attendance sheet going around the class. For a second, I just sat there, until I saw that Mrs. Gallo was very busy on the other side of the room with a student. I couldn't tell if she was answering a question or just chatting, but her back was to me. The room is really big. It can easily fit one hundred people. Six or seven rows of padded maroon seats with those tops that flip out if you want to use a book. Thinking quickly I grabbed my backpack and left the room unnoticed. I already signed in, so I won't lose anything for my attendance.

I did a little dance in the hallway once I was clear of the room and I knew that there was no way of me getting caught. A student walked and gave me a strange look as if she was too good for that sort of thing. Poor girl is so used to schools being boring that when she sees an idiot like me dancing, she walks the other way. Schools never allow students to have genuine fun, only controlled fun. Like at clubs or meetings, where you have to register, pay, and show ID beforehand to have a good time. I didn't care what anyone thought at that point. Screw the world. I'm dancing. I just got out of class with no penalty. That is a cause for celebration. And I'm pretty good at making myself look like an idiot anyway, so what's one more time really going to do to me; have people think I'm an idiot? It's too late for that. What? Will people think I'm more of an idiot? That doesn't even make sense.

This isn't the first time I pulled a stunt like that. In my freshmen year I took a marketing class, not because I wanted to, but because it was apart of the journalism requirements. I don't know who makes these requirements but it seems I'm taking every class other than actual journalism classes. We had a test and a lecture on the same day. Who doesn't love to sit in the room after answering a bunch of questions? I do. It's becoming a hobby of mine, along with sign making. Luckily for the class, the speaker was late, so you'd think that means we could get out early after the test. And you'd be wrong. The professor had us wait for the speaker to show. Like that was going to happen, I handed in the test and as soon as the teacher left the room, I was gone. I have better things to do then to listen to a speech by someone I don't know in a career that I'm not going into. I kind of got in trouble in the next class for leaving so soon. Not directly though. The teacher called out me and a few other students who left early, saying that we didn't receive attendance if we didn't stay for the speaker. That didn't bother me though.

I headed back over to the same table I sat at earlier with Moose in the small café. I managed to slip past the green people by going through the side door instead of the front. Moose was gone. The tarot reader was gone. The comedians were gone. In fact, everyone was gone. I was alone in the room. It would have been that way for longer if a few friends of mine didn't show up.

Paige and Natacha walked over shortly after I sat down. Paige has no idea what she wants to do for her career. Every time I see her she has a new major. One day she's a doctor, the next day a journalist, the next an actress. Today I say she's a nurse. Natacha has other problems. You know, like family problems. Something that you learn about in health class and you're not sure you want to know. I never asked her about what was going on at home, but I can tell she has a certain stress that Paige doesn't have to deal with. I bet someone in her family is a lot like Hemingway and I don't mean because of their writing.

I saw Paige first. She had on a light blue sweater with a cartoon penguin on it. She is from Sri Lanka. I don't know much about that place. It does sound like somewhere Mark Twain wrote about though. She said when I first met her that people think she is Indian, because that is what she looks like. She always wears glasses to cover up her cross-eyes. And she never mentioned it, but there is something wrong with her left forearm. It is too bony. I don't know what the problem is, but it's like she either has some disease, or she got into a really bad accident as a kid.

Natacha on the other hand doesn't have as many problems as Paige, physically at least. She has the body of stereotypical curvy black woman. I don't mean that as an insult. It's a compliment. She's in great shape, as she goes to the gym a lot. I know this since she mentioned it a few times. If you just looked at her, in her brown sweater with a yellow cat in the middle and her black pants, you wouldn't know something was wrong with her.

"Are you going to say hi?" Paige asked. I didn't want to talk. I just wanted to not be in class.

"Do you want me to say hi?" "Yeah."

"Well then hi."

"Sometimes you act so weird."

"Like you're normal."

They both sat down. Somehow neither of them chose the broken chair.

"I just don't know what to do," Paige said. "Should I change my major?"

I glanced at Natacha for some help on what Paige was talking about. "Last day to change majors is this Friday, so she has to decide soon if she wants to switch her major."

"Oh." I wasn't that caught up, but that was about as caught up as I was getting.

I tried to help. "Well, what do you want to do?"

"I don't know!"

What I meant was, what did she want to do in her life? What does she enjoy enough that she could do it as a job? Unfortunately, Paige is not smart enough to think on that kind of level. She sees it as a temporary problem.

"Maybe you should go to your advisor after class and tell her about it," Natacha said.

"What would you do?" Paige directed her question towards me.

I shrugged. "I'm a journalism major, so I'm fine."

"What does that mean? That you cover the news?"

"Well, it could. I could also write a book using that degree."

Natacha somehow took that as me saying that I'm writing a book. "I know what you should call your book." She paused for a second. "*'The Mind Of A Jackass.'*"

"That's not funny." Her mocking of my passion frustrated me a little, but I didn't let any of my emotions show.

"How about '*Week Of An Idiot*?'" Paige said with a smirk.

"Or '*Month Of A Moron*?'" They were enjoying this.

"'*Year Of The Imbecile*?'"

They both started laughing at my book comment.

"Seriously though. You should never write a book," Paige said. "You have to be, like, smart to do that. No offense."

I don't know why I even brought that up. It was stupid on my part. Not the dumbest thing I've ever said, but it's up there. Don't tell people about your dreams or your fears. Keep that shit to yourself. The truth is that nobody cares about your dream of being a writer or acting on Broadway or whatever other crap you want to do in your life. I hate to say it, but the world doesn't really give a shit about a dream you have that will probably never come true. So am I really writing a novel? Am I really trying to be a comedian? No. Not at all.

Natacha then went on about how awful school was. Like none of us know that already. Neither Paige nor me said anything. Apparently Natacha is not doing so well, in every class. I don't know if it's her study habits or if she's just plain stupid, but school is not working out for her.

"You know some of these teachers are so dumb." She had a particular problem with the professor for our next class, Miss Wello and her teaching habits. Probably how quick attendance gets done. "She doesn't know what she's talking about. Oh my god, if I have to hear another story about a kid in Africa, I am going to flip. I mean, I can teach the class. Give me a degree and let me speak in front of students about donating and famine."

I couldn't take her complaining anymore. I don't need to be reminded of how much I hate a class before I get to the actual class. "You know, while we're at it let's complain about your shoes being too tight, or the temperature in the classroom being too hot, or the lunch line being too damn long." I was on a roll. "Let me see, I can complain about the seat I'm sitting in, the books I carry, the posters on the wall."

She cut me off. "I'm not complaining."

"You just sound like you were complaining." I do that sometimes. Come to think of it, I am not cursing at all in this book. No. Not one bit. I just sound like I'm cursing. There's a big difference.

"She's counting me for nine absences even though I registered late for the class."

I changed to a more serious tone "Can she do that?"

"Well, she did. She's such a bitch. Feminist my ass!"

"You know I was late for a bunch of classes too. I hope she didn't mark me absent for them," Paige said. If there is one thing we all have in common, it's tardiness.

I chimed in, "Next time you can't make it, tell her that somebody in your family died and you're going to the funeral."

"I'm not doing that," Natacha said.

"Sure, because telling your professor that you're too lazy sounds real great."

Paige asked, "You would lie to your professor and say that your grandpa died?"

"Of course not," I quickly responded. "I already used that excuse."

I did. Last year, I lied to a professor saying that my grandpa died and that I would miss class because of the wake, but really I just didn't want to go to the early class. Later that same day, who do I see when walking to another class? That same professor who I lied to in the email. She didn't say anything as I walked by, but she probably put two and two together. If you want to get sympathy from a teacher, use a death in the family. What? Are they going to call you out on it? Claim that you're fabricating it? No. Because no one wants to be that much of an asshole. Sure using death as an excuse is low, but trying to call someone out who you think is using death as an excuse is even lower.

I didn't lie when I said I lost my grandpa. I did. Just not last year. It was about ten years ago. God, has it been that long? I lost him and my grandma the same week that year. That was a tough week. Tough birthday too. I don't remember much about it. Just that I never saw so many people cry and never dressed so fancy in my life. Funny how people look their best when they are a wreck. I've been to a bunch of funerals since. Now death doesn't really bother me. Also everyone in my family died the same month as my grandparents: my mom's brother, my aunt, my uncle, my other aunt, my other uncle, my cousin, and my other cousin. When I die, I'll probably die in February.

Paige then started to tell us about her major. Which as I said, changes every day. She talked for like ten minutes about her choices and how she doesn't know if she should switch majors, if it's too late to switch majors. There's also a class that she wants to drop, but she doesn't know if she can now. Unfortunately for her, she didn't talk to someone who knows about the deadline date to drop classes. Ugh... Paige can really go on and on. Natacha and I probably could have gotten some coffee and sat back down and Paige would have still been talking. But we listened to her rant because she apparently didn't like our advice. Why can't people skip to the parts of the story that they think you should care about instead of talking for ten minutes and getting nowhere with the topic?

People should only talk about what they know, which means most shouldn't talk at all. Luckily for Natacha and I, the three of us soon went over to our History of Inequality class.

I'll admit that I didn't look at the class description when I signed up for it. All I did was get screwed by the person making the schedule. The same one who let Moose have off for the rest of the day. I guess I thought the class was more of a history course. It's not. We talk about how woman do not have as many rights as men in every class, which makes me even more uncomfortable since I'm the only boy in the class. Most of the topics we discuss point out the awful things that men do to control and oppress women. Turns out men are pretty savage. I don't want to defend men because there are some situations I can't defend. I can only defend my own actions. Not some stranger that I never met in my entire life. Add to that my two friends always sit next to me interrupting any conversations I have with other girls, and the class where I'm the only guy is not as great as you'd think. As everyone talks about inequality, I'm writing whatever jokes I can think of on whatever paper I am given.

Miss Wello teaches this class. She's a small middle-aged woman with blonde hair that is never set. She's always nervous too, as if she just came from a hospital. She has a good heart though and wants to change the world, feed all the starving children, get equal rights for all, yet she can't even get her life together. She's late for her own class and has on an outfit that looks like she bought it from a flea market and hasn't cleaned it since. And people think I'm full of contradictions. Examine yourself long enough and I'm sure you'll find you're as bad as Miss Wello or me.

When she stumbled into class, she put her huge brown bag on the desk. The bag was bigger than her. Probably calmer. I guess carrying around one is a requirement for changing the world. In it was a stack of folders that if they were in my room, I'd say, "Yeah. I'm not bothering with all that."

"Oh my God, can you believe the parking lot?" she said, shuffling through the folders. "I, no lie, had to walk across the entire campus to get here. That's why I'm so late. Someone should do something about that." As if none of us know about the bad parking on campus.

A student close to her turned to respond, not because she wanted to, but because she was a foot away from her. I believe her name is Samantha. I don't talk to her. She always sits right by the door though. The type of girl who talks because she's a nice person. She doesn't actually care about the fact that Miss Wello was late. If she was in the back part of the room, she'd have said nothing and continued to check her phone. She is full of shit when it comes to her selection in guys too. She says she likes guys who are respectful and kind and caring, yet she'll date a jerk. I know this because she has brought up to the class how she has fights with him over stupid stuff. She's smart enough to know a jerk, but not smart enough to leave one. One of the benefits of being in an all-girl class is I get to hear them all complain about their boyfriends. Lucky me. I would have dropped this class by now, but it is too late, so I am stuck with it.

Anyway, she answered with a simple, "I know, right?"

Since Miss Wello was so occupied by the folders, she didn't take the cue to shut up. "How do they expect people to be on time for class if the parking lot is always full?"

Samantha said quietly, "I don't know," and Miss Wello took out a paper for attendance. "For those of you who weren't here last class, we had Joanne, Sabrina, and Jennifer give a presentation to the class on barbaric abortions." Let me say this, for those of you who missed last class; smart decision on your part because we had to sit through gruesome ways women don't have babies. To think I actually showed up.

I feel bad for them for even having to present something. Jennifer, the brains of the group, did most of the talking. She may have done the whole presentation and let the other two give enough info so that they can pass too. Joanne and Sabrina, who are on the lacrosse team, just added facts that they didn't really understand, but knew they should read. Jennifer saved them by appearing interested in her research. She and Miss Wello went back and forth about the topic for a few minutes. This made it appear like they all cared about it. Jennifer may have. As for the other two, they were there because they had to.

What do I have to present? Nothing. It was randomly assigned to the three girls. No one else had to speak. I really hope that I don't have to ever do a presentation for this class. Not because I hate public speaking, but because I really hate doing group presentations. I have to get together with other students. We have to decide what type of presentation we want to do. We have to assign roles for it. Then we have to do it. The whole thing is a lot of work for a topic I will forget by next semester.

It takes forever to take attendance in the class. I'm not kidding when I say it took half the class to complete. Which I'm not complaining about. If there's one thing I learned in school, it's never rush attendance and don't ask too many questions. Attendance can make the class seem shorter since the teacher won't talk as much about the topic, whether it's about the end of the world or barbaric abortions. Asking questions may lead the teacher to going over the time limit. Never ask questions if you want to get out on time.

Teachers love to say that attendance and homework are important. Or that participation is key to your grade. Because now that the teacher said that raising my hand is essential, I will definitely raise my hand for the whole semester. Yeah, right.

Actually, two or three classes ago I lied about reading the assignment we discussed in class. Miss Wello asked the class the typical question all teachers ask about the reading assignment, *"What did you get from reading last class's assignment?"* and I had a good response; I quoted the line at the top of the first chapter of the book. It was by Lincoln and had to do with asking a slave about enjoying that lifestyle. Once I said that, I was off the hook. It appeared like I read the four chapters we were assigned. I didn't. I just memorized that one line and she bought it.

The classroom is pretty congested. You can barely get around the small black desks positioned in the room. The twenty of us are on top of each other, even when we move the desks. It's always cold in the room when we first enter since the window is constantly left open. One of the girls who sit by it normally closes it.

As Miss Wello attempted to go through attendance, we moved the desks around as much as we could so that we were in a circle. Natacha was on the outside of it since we had no room for all the desks.

Then we finally got to the actual lesson. We passed around a picture of a woman who got raped and then hung in the town square. Messed up stuff. Like real sick shit. Apparently people do that all the time over there. I don't remember where the picture was taken from exactly. I'd bet a country that I couldn't locate or pronounce, possibly both.

How come by the time we notice harmful things in the world, it's too late? Like that poor woman in the picture. My god. She did nothing to be treated like that. I guess the problem is not that she did nothing wrong, it's that the others thought what they were doing was right. And we call this the Information Age. Pathetic.

There were other pictures of similar disturbing acts. Each image had a line under the horror scene. *"BECAUSE SHE SPOKE UP" "BECAUSE SHE WANTED TO GO TO SCHOOL" "BECAUSE SHE DIDN'T LIKE HER*

HUSBAND" I don't want to describe anything else about the images to you. Even if I could, they are too much for someone too handle.

Do you see why I don't pay attention to half of what goes in this class? Now can you understand why I was staring at the paper and writing whatever I could think of instead of participating? Anything besides listening to Miss Wello talk about messed up murder victims and the inequality in the world.

My deflection didn't stop her though. Miss Wello spoke once we all saw the black and white images. "Are you not mad about this? This makes me pissed. Because this is wrong. And I won't live in a world where this takes place." Her philosophy is that if you are not mad about the world then you aren't paying attention. She's said it multiple times during classes about varying human rights issues. It fits into her missionary approach to life. She's even a donor to a kid from another country.

She held up the image with the marriage tagline. "Just…just look at this one. Do you think this is right? Women being burned for not wanting to marry a guy? I don't. If I can't choose to marry who I want to marry, then I'm not marrying at all."

The class discussion went on and classmates went on and on about the abuse women in other countries have to deal with and how they are not even viewed as equals in some parts of the world.

Miss Wello then took out a piece of chalk and asked the class to shout some derogatory words for women.

As girls called out inappropriate words like slut, and whore or cunt, Miss Wello wrote them on the board. Then after filling half the board with at least twenty words to insult women, she asked the same question for men. The class came up with five, if that many.

Surprisingly Sabrina, the lacrosse player who acts like she never wants to be in class, told everyone how she feels like everyone is watching her when she walks in the room. "Guys, they even have a phrase for it. They say they hit that. Like women are objects."

Miss Wello sat down on the front desk. "I know, and they act like we are only there for their pleasure. Like

I am only here to make you like how I look. Honey, I am staying healthy and fit for my own life, not yours."

Sabrina spoke like she has been meaning to tell someone this, but never had the chance "I don't like how I know in locker rooms that's what guys are saying about me."

At one point Miss Wello even called me out to ask for my opinion. I am a guy, I must have something useful to add to the conversation that is about the two genders. "What do you think Nick? Have you ever felt like the room was looking at you when you entered it?"

"No." I kept it short since I didn't know what to say. I didn't want to participate.

Miss Wello then got back up and pointed to the board. "You see these words. All these words hurt us. We allow men to call us these. And we even call ourselves these. I can't tell you how many times I have called a woman a bitch. And do you know what that does? Do you know what it can lead to? This." She held up one of gruesome photos of a dead woman. "If we do not respect ourselves to stand up to insults that men give us, then we will one day be in a world where this is acceptable. I refuse to live in such a world."

The only thing that saved me was the time. All of a sudden she looked at her watch and called out to the room, "Oh my God. Class is over in five minutes. Let's put the desks back to their original spots."

And just like that, the class was over. We repositioned the desks and left.

The three of us, meaning Natacha, Paige, and I, headed back to the plaza, but we never got back to the café because we saw a great friend of mine. Someone that I am sure you know very well. He's on the school's site in one of those goofy pictures where they have students planting a tree or whatever other bullshit to show school support. Does he cover events like Midnight Madness? No. He's too good for that. He's covering more relevant events on campus that only he could investigate. He's in history club because he knows so much about history. He's in the science club because he knows so much about science. He throws the biggest parties while being in charge of the prohibition club. He's in twenty different organizations and, oh yeah, he works too. He's interning for a big business company in the city. Of course he is. The dean knows him by name and everyone laughs when he makes a joke even if it's not funny. When he tells people that he's thinking about being a comedian, they encourage him to go for it. Even though he has never gone on stage in his life. He is the guy women cheat with. He has a schmuck smile that makes me want to punch him. I truly hate this man. He doesn't act on things because he believes in what he's doing but because he knows people are watching him. He's full of shit. And what do I hate the most about him? That I'm the idiot with this. I'm the moron here. Because you, you all love this man. You will give him more awards than he'll ever deserve. Give him more accolades than he should get. You will put him on a pedestal by displaying him on the wall in the communications building before he even does anything. He can do no wrong. Until it turns out that the darling is involved in drug dealing and is accused of raping a girl. Even then people will side with him.

His name is Joe. Mike? Scott? I don't know, and I really don't want to find out. He can go to hell for all I care.

"Oh my God, it's been so long!" Natacha ran over and gave him a hug. Not long enough, if you ask me.

I ignored The Jerk as he bragged to Natacha and Paige about his great schooling experience. If I listen to his bullshit for too long, I just may have to kill him.

As I was pretending to listen I reached into my pocket to find the paper I ripped down about the writing meeting. I examined it a little bit. I still couldn't go because of my fourth class with the great writer Mr. Richard.

"So you want to go?" The Jerk asked me.

"Hmmm?" I didn't know what he was talking about.

"To eat. The three of us are going to eat."

Paige brought up my future publishing career. "Nah. He's too busy writing that great novel to go out with us. Aren't you?"

"I could be."

"Come on. Want to go?"

"No. I can't. I have another class."

As the three of them walked toward the parking lot, Paige turned around and called out, "Bye Mick!" Good to know I make a difference in their lives.

The world has gone cool with all the edited videos and fake profiles and promotions and bullshit. We say that looks mean nothing but judge each other as soon as we can. Don't give your book a cover and see how many of them will give it a glance. I don't know. It's just...sometimes I can't help but wonder if one of these days I shouldn't wake up when I drive home. That may be the only way for the world to even notice I'm here. Being in a tragedy could be the most attention I ever get in my life. Cause right now, no one seems to care that I'm here. There's always someone else picked that society would rather have than me. As if I'm not good enough. A better writer, a funnier comedian, a better student, a more creative story. The world doesn't want guys like me. They're just waiting for me to step aside and give up so that the ones they really want come along. People who march along to the drums they're playing, who do as they're told. Not me. Even if I do succeed, people will want me to fail since I don't belong, according to them, or they will kiss my ass, because they're so shocked that I'm even alive. Hard work? Honesty? Keep lying to yourself that those traits are important. We lie to ourselves enough, I'm sure one more lie can't hurt. You don't need integrity or any of that other bullshit that you're told about for success. You'll go far in this world if you learn how to lie with a pretty smile. As for me, maybe I belong with the open mic crowd more than I'd care to admit.

I continued to scan the paper as I waited for them to be out of sight. Nothing on it was useful. You'd figure that out of all the signs, the writing one would be the most descriptive. You'd be wrong. It didn't even include an exact time. It just said *"AFTERNOON."*

Sitting on a bench in the plaza was my next-door neighbor Kathleen. I knew she went to the school since my mom told me about it a while back. I just never followed through with reaching out to her. She was much more attractive than I remember her being. Which may sound great, but the last time I saw her we were in high school and she was goth. Now she was all cleaned up. She didn't get prettier, but she wasn't wearing all black and frowning all the time. The angst she used to have was gone. Most of it at least. You don't get rid of angst. You transfer that energy towards something else.

"Oh hey," She was surprised to see me. "How's it going?"

"Good. How about you?" I continued to stand.

"Good. Good." It was at this point when I saw the instrument case on the bench next to her, so I asked her about it. If I had said nothing then, I would have been talking to Damian all over again.

"You're a musician." I pointed to the case. I vaguely remember seeing her walk around high school with an instrument. Don't ask me which. I don't know. It's one that you can fit into a carry case, if that helps (it probably doesn't).

"Oh. No. I'm becoming a music teacher."

"Oh." I was taken back that someone my age would want to do that. I thought most music majors wanted to be professional musicians. I mean, I don't want to become a writing teacher right now. "Good for you."

"Yeah." You could tell she didn't know what to say. Neither did I. We were both just being nice. "How about you?"

"I'm taking journalism classes."

"Wow, that's great." In other words, I don't know what that means, but since we are sort of friends I have to pretend to be interested.

We said our goodbyes and acted like we would see each other again soon. We won't though.

I headed over to the communications building. When I walked inside I saw a stack of newspapers in a bin that hasn't been touched, and I walked past the esteemed wall of shame, I mean fame. On the door of the classroom was a sign that said that class was canceled. The right class this time.

The teacher of the canceled class is Mr. Richard and he doesn't teach us anything in Newspaper Writing. He just assigns us various topics to write about and then grades them. His lessons consist of him somehow mentioning whatever writing career he had or somehow relating the material to his own perspective. Like how he would write it, since that's what we all want to know. He told us how he wrote a book about a murder that was a big deal when it happened. At least according to him. I bet he thought that was his ticket to literary fame. The great teacher thinks so much of his writing that he brings sample articles of what he wrote when he was younger since he thought we would like to read it. I'm not kidding. He isn't like the German composer with his attitude, since he's a mellow guy, but he doesn't know how to shut up about his mediocre writing.

When he isn't boring us with nostalgia, he's rambling on about writing, like it has some great purpose in life, like there is some higher calling we are all achieving by reporting on a sports game. He'd say something like, "Do your words capture a time, a people, a feel? Do they give the reader all they need to know of the culture? Do your words take the readers through the lives of the people who live there, show them the lifestyle, the good and the bad?

Are your words more than words?" That's one of his many rants on the significance of literature and prose for human society.

Which actually, let me see, last time I checked, my words are still just words. Oh, look at that, they still are.

For some reason, when I saw the sign I said something I'd hear on a commercial. "This moment is brought to you by…WOOOH! No class! Good! I don't even like this class. I was going to drop it anyway."

I don't know why I said that. I don't plan on dropping the class. I can't. It's part of my requirements for being a journalism major.

Benny, in his high-pitched voice, said, "You can't drop the class. The last day to drop was last Friday." Who is Benny to me? Harry's stupid, more annoying cousin. He raises his hand every two seconds. Why? Because he just has to put his two cents in every conversation, even when we all know that he has no clue what he's talking about.

"Oh. Then I'm not dropping it." Dude, shut the fuck up. I'm celebrating over no class and this asshole is telling me I'm wrong. He probably has everything planned for his great future too. He has that great internship that will get him a job. He already paid for his parking sticker, and he actually studies when he's not given homework. This guy thinks that by getting straight A's, he'll be better equipped for the real world. Moron.

I wasn't going into a full-blown explanation on how I misspoke and said that only because I hated the class. I was done for the day with classes. As far as I'm concerned, I have to leave before the teacher shows up.

Two other students witnessed the exchange but said nothing. I don't know their names. One is the hot chick in the class and the other is the stoner, because that's what they look like to me. Sorry, but I don't have any other description for them, since you know, I am not their friends and all I can see from them is their appearance. The hot chick looks like a model with her blonde hair and blue eyes. And the stoner looks high with his messy hair and blood shot eyes. For one, you wonder what she looks like naked, and for the other, you wonder what he looks like sober. Wondering is the most I will ever get to know about these too. Neither of them reacted to the exchange between Benny and me.

I remembered the writing meeting, so with my newfound time I headed on over to the science building.

The best part about these stupid meetings, besides the amazing signs, is the food. I've gone to enough writing meetings that I learned not to go for the talent. This is my first time going to this writing meeting though. Poetry slams are like that too. You think that they're better than they really are. But they kind of suck. You sit there for God knows how long listening to wannabe poets recite their pieces just to read your one poem. Which, let's be honest, isn't all that great either. I actually hope that no one ever reads the poems that I wrote for the slams I went to. They were pretty dumb. Of course, now I say that. When I'm on stage, my poem is amazing. When you're there, don't expect a young Mark Twain, William Shakespeare, or whoever it is that you think is a talented writer, to read a sonnet-to-be. You won't be hearing the first draft of "The Raven" at a poetry slam. Believe me when I say that if you ever have to go, then go for the food, not the actual writing. A cookie and a cup of coffee is the best thing you'll get at a poetry slam.

It was a smaller meeting than I imagined, only me and four other students. Oh, who am I kidding? It was the exact size I expected. I'm talking about a writing meeting, not a football game. The room itself was not much larger than someone's office. There was a small table in the center of the room with a couch and some chairs around it. On the table was a plate of cookies.

The woman speaking was sitting upright in one of the chairs, practically sliding off the edge. She was about forty and looked like an alien. Like she may go home later tonight and transform into her natural form. She looks human enough to pass, but that's it. The other leader of the meeting was standing behind the counter in the office away from the rest of us. She was about sixty, had short gray hair, and didn't say much during the meeting. All she did was focus her attention on the meeting. And no, I don't think she was an alien. Two other people my age were sitting in the chairs available. I don't have much to say about them, since I mostly listened to the alien woman when I first sat down. As she spoke, I wondered whether I got extra credit for going, but I didn't want to ask about it. I reached for a cookie and a small plate as the alien woman continued to talk.

A girl with glasses sat next to me on the couch and was writing in her notebook. I don't know what she could be writing. We weren't talking about anything worth remembering. I can't even begin to speculate what she was jotting down.

The alien woman went on for another five minutes before ending the meeting. "We have another meeting next week." She stood up and erased some facts on pons that were on the white board. Don't ask. I don't know what a pon is either. In its place were the words *"Next week's meeting same time, same place."*

What was the meeting actually about? Good question. I'm trying to figure that one out too. What are any writing meetings about? As far as I can tell they don't have any true purpose. The women probably needed a reason to get rid of the cookies

and they didn't want to have a bake sale. I'm not sure
if they know this, but writing meetings don't actually
help your writing. I didn't ask any questions during it.
When I am in a situation like that, I don't say
anything. I sit still and let people talk to see how much
they can say until they start bullshitting me and they
run out of premeditated lines. See, they expect me to
participate and ask questions and be eager to join.
They aren't prepared for a guy who just sits down in
the meeting, eats some cookies, and says nothing.
People will continue to talk and talk to fill the silence,
sometimes saying things that they don't mean to say,
which is what I want to hear. Not them reciting crap I
can read in a pamphlet. Apparently there is some new
writing program that the school is trying out and they
need to see if any students would join. Going by the
large numbers that showed up, I'd say no. I told you
the food was the best part.

This isn't the first time I went to an after-school
event. Once, I kid you not, I went to Bible study. I was
in the café late one night keeping to myself, when a
pretty girl asked if I wanted to join her Bible study
group. Of course I said yes. I'm a college guy and she
was cute. She could have asked me anything and I'd
have said yes. Me, the girl, whose name is Katrina,
and her friend, whose name I don't know, and some
other person, were the only ones in the group. This is
not to imply that she sought out great men like
myself. She went up to every person sitting in the
café. I was the only one who accepted her offer. You

know Bible study groups are desperate when they're asking biblical scholars like me to sit in.

What do I know about the Bible? Not much. I never took my after-school Catholic classes seriously. I drew doodles in the book. It was only after taking the classes that I realized some of the stuff is actually used in the real world. All I know is that one line in that book is more influential than everything I have told you so far. I can't name another book that affected the world so much.

The Bible study group was exactly what you thought it would be. We read passages from the book and then asked questions about what we read. It was like school, but even more boring. I'm the worst when it comes to answering questions about spirits and religion. I hope there isn't a quiz to get into heaven.

After reading a passage, Katrina asked the group a question to stimulate a conversation. "What do you think God is trying to say about Satan in this passage? Is there anything God is trying to warn us of him?"

No one said anything. Katrina turned to me as if to get me to talk. It worked. "Well I, ah, if I were the Devil, I'd get people to like my minions, or those who obey me. All the people in the spotlight would work for me. Not openly though. They would never bring me up in public, but behind closed doors they'd seek my guidance." I continued to talk nonsense. "God wants you to believe in Him. The Devil wants you to worship him. I think there's a difference."

No one knew what to say after my silly rambling. Katrina quickly asked the rest of the group for any other interpretations, being that mine was so off. I stopped our conversation before it got started.

That's nothing compared to what I said at another Bible study. Okay, so I have gone to two Bible studies in my life. This group was much larger than the other group. I'd say there were about twenty people in the meeting. Katrina was there too. This time there was pizza. She must have learned from the poetry slams about giving people food. In the meeting was a young pastor, no more than thirty years old, and he enjoyed talking to people about their problems more than actually solving anything. He had a business card and gave everyone his phone number in case we needed to talk to him and praying wasn't enough. Once the meeting started, he asked us to describe our fear.

A girl said, "I'll admit that I don't have much faith in God." For some reason, people who doubt God love to tell the world about it. "I mean, I want to believe, but I don't even know why I should."

"You fear that your faith in God serves you no purpose," the pastor said.

She was noticeably upset. "Yeah. I'm paying the bills. I'm working. I'm studying and going to classes. Like, what has God done for me lately? 'Cause it seems to me that it's me doing all the work." She had a point. I didn't see God carry that pizza pie over here.

"You must remember that a truly great life is not one filled with money and fame, but with love. And how do you find love? Through God. He will see your good soul and allow you into the kingdom of heaven as long as you keep Him with you and remember that He gave up His own son for you. And that son, Jesus Christ, died for your sins. Now, you and many here may question God. Do not ask what can God do for you. Ask what you can do to be closer to God?" Despite his best efforts, the girl didn't buy it, but she didn't want to start a fight over the philosophical purpose of a higher power over pizza and soda.

Next was me. I once again didn't give the right answer. I told the group that I have trust issues. That no matter what happens at the meeting, I will find a reason to leave the place alone. I never let anyone too close out of fear that I will lose them. I have created a barrier so that I never hurt anyone or get hurt by anyone. I can't have a broken heart if I never let anyone in.

The pastor was shocked by my response. "Wow. That is a man who knows himself." And he asked the next person in line about their fear. He didn't try to offer his help to me.

Pastors don't know what to do when you know more about yourself than they do. Also, people get freaked out when you say too much about yourself. It's like people want to know you, but not too well. Whenever someone asks how you're doing, they want to hear an amusing anecdote, maybe about a conversation you had with some friends or about something that happened on your ride to work. Not your real fears. They don't want to hear that. I say "real fears" because I don't mean the fake fears you put on a form in a questionnaire, like heights or spiders. No. I'm talking about the fears that really scare you. The ones that no one likes to talk about. The ones that only you know. Want people to think you're strange? Bring up a real deep personal fear you have to them. They won't look at you the same afterwards, even though they have a fear just as deep, and just as personal.

I don't want to come across as some noble saint or whatever since I went to Bible study groups. That's not the case. Sometimes for no reason at all I have messed up thoughts. Does that ever happen to you? Randomly you will think of some disturbing, sick thing that no one wants to hear. Like your desire to kill someone or steal. Of course, I know the thoughts are wrong to act on. I'm not a complete psychopath. But sometimes I don't mind seeing people suffer. Watching them cry, seeing pain in their eyes. There's something poetic about tragedy. Oh boy, looks like I forgot to tell the group a few things.

After the writing meeting, if you even want to call it that, I walked back towards the plaza, hoping to see Kathleen again. I felt like I wanted to talk to her more.

Maybe about her music preferences, or just to see how her family was doing. I don't know what we would have talked about, but I really wanted to talk to her. Which is weird since, like I told you, I'm not even her friend. Sometimes the people you want in your life the most at that moment are never there at all.

Needless to say, she wasn't there. No one was. There was only a sign promoting all the upcoming events at the theater. Like anybody besides the students involved care about them. Those events are no different than Midnight Madness; the school has to make it seem bigger than it actually is. Do schools think that students walk around and rip down flyers that they find interesting? I guess all the music majors with their instruments and dreams were in their classes learning how to make each other laugh and quit their bands.

Musicians have an arrogance about them I can't stand. They think they are so cool because they can play whatever piece of crap they carry around. As if they are this music prodigy. They all believe they are so gifted that the world just needs to hear them. I wouldn't be surprised if John Cage was a musician. He has an attitude like that too.

I had no more reasons to be on campus, so I headed to my car.

As I walked back to my car, I saw a familiar face. John Cage was sitting by his artwork, if you want to call it that. While you're calling the rock a piece of art, go ahead and call this story an adventure.

God, don't these artists ever give up? Your art is underappreciated. Get over it. No one cares that your rock is really a symbol for the betrayal one feels while living in the world, or whatever dumbass explanation you have behind it. Someone should tell artists that no one reads books for the multiple-choice questions.

"Hey, what're you doing?" he called out to me.

"What does it look like I'm doing? I'm walking." I have some charm. It's no wonder I'm so trustworthy. It may look like I'm just walking, but I'm really going out of my way to slay a dragon and save the day. It's like the parts of the story that you hate. You don't hate them, you just think you hate them. There is a difference. Obviously.

"You shouldn't walk on the grass." All of a sudden the artist follows the rules. It's fine when he makes art that has no logic to it though.

"Whatever." I kept walking. I'm only good for one philosophical question a day. After that, I lose interest in questioning the world. That's my big complaint about philosophy; too much talking and not enough doing. How many questions does a philosopher have to ask before they actually do something?

It took me a freaking year to get back to my car since I parked it on another freaking planet. When I got there, I saw four blue cars that were exactly alike lined up in a row. I stopped for a second to see if my eyes were right. They were. Four identical cars were all in a row. I laughed at the absurdity behind it. Just when life starts making sense, when the story starts to go somewhere, you see some weird thing that you can't explain.

My laughter didn't last long as I found a ticket for not having a parking sticker for my car. Sixty dollars. Can you believe that? Sixty dollars just to park a million miles away from the school. For what? A lousy education, some bad food, and ignorant teachers? Screw that. I crumbled up the ticker and threw it into my car. Sorry Mom. Car stickers are another reason I hate this goddamn place.

Want to know how I'm doing financially? Look at my damn ticket. What? Do you want me to write an economic paper on how I have no money? Do you want me to give you a pie chart explaining why I have nothing in my wallet? Get the hell out of here. I'm broke. That's all you need to know. The system looked at me and my generation and said, "You know what? I really want to take everything from them. Give them low paying jobs, high costs on education, and no guaranteed retirement." They tell me it isn't about the money but about my future, how I will contribute to the world, and there's so much for me to do. Yet they take every dollar they can from me. Universities are nothing more than businesses today. And they love guys like The Jerk. Why? Because he gets them in the news in a positive light. Which means more money for them.

As I drove home, I felt very sleepy, probably because I am such a hard working student. Seriously though, I shouldn't have been driving. To prevent myself from passing out, I turned on the AC full blast and cranked the radio up.

If I wasn't so exhausted, I would have listened to one of those great sports radio shows. 'Cause those guys always know what they are talking about. Yeah, and I'm a real comedian and this story has a plot. Sure. Like one time a host said, and I quote, "I'm rooting harder than ever in my life." How the hell do you root harder than someone? Do you wear your jerseys more than me? Do you attend more games than me? Memorize more statistics? What does that even mean? I might as well say I am writing harder than ever before. Sure, why not? Makes just as much sense.

I wanted to listen to music on the ride so that the jams could keep me awake. I feel I can stay awake longer if I'm blasting cold air in my face and have music in my ears. I have the perfect song to keep me going too. Commercials, which sadly enough have some of the best songs on the radio.

That kept me awake long enough to get home. Kind of. About four or five times while driving, on the highway, no less, I passed out briefly. I'd wake up and be a few feet further in the lane than I was before, which is why I didn't bother changing the channel. I don't suggest ever driving like this, unless you want to get into a car accident. Then go right ahead. I'll save a tree for you. You may get lucky and have an orange ambulance pick you up. I'm actually surprised I haven't died in a car accident yet. Between my shitty car and sleepy driving, I should not be on the road most times. For some reason, my ride home seemed like it took shorter than my ride to school. Probably because I was so out of it.

As I drove down my block, I saw an old neighbor, Miss Rasperman, leaving her house. She used to have a big Halloween party at her house that the whole block would attend. She stopped doing it after her husband died about six years ago. I didn't wave as I drove by because I knew she wouldn't recognize me. The last time we spoke, she was giving me candy.

Part 4 – Home 2

I locked my car and was about to head inside when I saw my next-door neighbor, Matt, standing at the curb of our driveway. I used to hang out with him as a kid. We lost touch in high school even though he's only a year older than me and we both lived in the same houses for those years. I stopped and said hello. There was no way of avoiding him. I expected my old friend to give me a quick answer, maybe a "sup" or a "hey," even a small wave would do, so that way I could get on with my day, but he didn't. Apparently he just finished working out and wanted to share his dream of being a police officer with yours truly.

He even told me how he's going to apply to be a cop. To which I brought up my college days in journalism. Nothing particular like the professors or classes. Just that I was taking journalism. He wasn't impressed, but he wasn't disappointed either. He took it like he didn't know if it was good or bad. Probably because he was sweating so much. I bet if I told him I was in the newspaper club, he'd be impressed. Those irrelevant articles that fill the pages of the paper in the bin don't write themselves. I didn't even bring up my comedy to him, since no one thinks that I'm funny anyway. I confuse people when I tell them I want to be a comedian. They look at me like I said something wrong. As if I gave them wrong directions and they know I gave them wrong directions. He then went on for fifteen minutes about going to the academy, how he can do this, do that because of the potential job, blah, blah, blah. I didn't want to be rude and interrupt, but he could have saved me about fourteen minutes of talking.

Most guys my age that take the police officer test only do it because they're too stupid to do much of anything else. They know all they have to do is get into shape and study for it and they could be in, since a million freaking people apply for the test. Once they pass, they can wait for their name to be called. If you look at the guys in your class who became police officers, chances are they weren't the ones you'd pick. They were kind of stupid while in school. I can name four or five guys from my high school class who are becoming cops. None of them have a brain. I won't even make a comparison to Sherlock Holmes here, since that's giving them too much credit. Let's face it; if you were smarter, you'd be a scientist. If you were tougher, you'd be a soldier. If you had a talent, you'd be an artist. And if you had a good heart, you'd be a pastor. But no, you became a cop. Because that's the only thing you could do.

Matt fits the profile perfectly. He was never one of the smartest on the block. Of the two of them, Kasey had more brains. If you can believe this, Matt has a younger brother with an even lower IQ than him. I know, it's difficult to fathom. I told you that everyone I know is stupid. Matt was all juiced up on steroids too. You could tell he had been taking them since his muscles were the size of my head. Some guys are just big boned. Like me. My shoulders are much bigger than the average person my height, so I could take steroids and not look bad. Matt can't. He has too frail of a frame that being so ripped makes him look like a caricature. It's like he went to an artist and asked, "Can you make a picture of me with steroids?"

This guy is the closest thing I ever had to a brother growing up. Not sure why that matters. But you should know that we weren't always strangers. I didn't always avoid him when I saw him. At one point in our youth, we were friends. We played video games together, had sleepovers, all the stuff that kids love to do. That was before life got in the way, I guess. I'm not sure what happened exactly. Years went by and all of a sudden the last I spoke to him was when we were in elementary school. Now we barely talk. The short talk I had with him is the most I'll see him until one day I learn that he moved to another state because of a job offer.

I looked to get a bite to eat as soon as Matt was done talking and I was inside the house. I checked the fridge to find the leftover Chinese food Mom spoke about. There was not much left, just some rice, my Kung Pao Chicken, and other Chinese food that was not mine. Some chicken that I never eat. The containers of Kung Pao and rice seemed like enough for me, so I put them in the microwave for two minutes. I can never decide what to do when I have to wait for something in the microwave. Should I stand there for the two minutes counting the seconds? Maybe I can put on the TV in the kitchen and catch some of Dan Isles's acting. Sometimes I even try to do the dishes since the sink is right next to the microwave. I don't know why, but I always feel like I have to do something. In the time I was fretting, the rice and Kung Pao chicken were reheated. I pulled out a plate from the cupboard, put the leftovers on it, and sat down at the kitchen table to begin eating. I say begin, because I ate too fast and got heartburn. That is a pain in your chest, for those of you who never had one. The first time you have heartburn, you think you are having a heart attack. You aren't though, just heartburn. When I got heartburn, I didn't do anything for the first minute or so, thinking it would pass. This one didn't though. It was bad. I looked in the medicine cabinet by the fridge and of course, we had no heartburn medicine, so I decided to wait it out. But it was way worse than I thought it would be. I tried to drink water, but it came right back out. For a second time I searched for some medicine and I found something and—I threw it back up. I was doing real bad. I just kept spitting and spitting into the sink in the bathroom. My whole mouth was watering. I must have been in there for fifteen minutes heeling over the sink and toilet. When I wasn't spitting in the sink, I threw up whatever I ate in the toilet. The rice, the chicken, it all came back up. About ten minutes through, I thought I would die because of the whole thing. Nothing could go down. I was putting my heart and body through hell and I may not make it out alive.

Luckily for you and more importantly me, it did stop. It was such a shame that I didn't die then since I was really looking forward to all those poems being handed out at my wake. I'll chalk them one up to a missed chance. Maybe in the next story I'll write. I didn't eat after that incident. My eyes were red, my pores were dripping sweat, and I felt like I would pass out, as if I had been the one working out. For a few minutes I sat motionless at the computer table by the front door, trying to regain my energy.

I didn't even fully grasp my surroundings when I reached into my backpack for the paper with my jokes. I was still a little woozy but I no longer had any pain and I got some energy back. Not much energy. Enough to sit still. I didn't want to go to the comedy club with a piece of paper that I couldn't read. I'll be up on stage marking off what the audience thinks is funny and by the time I get to my third joke I can't even read the paper. Is that a V or a W? I don't know. My paper is all messy. After awhile all the cross-outs and rewrites confuse me so much that I forget what I wrote. Which sucks if I wrote some great line. I don't worry about that too much though.

I turned on the computer, opened up a Word Document, and tried my best to put whatever notes I could understand on the document. I did a pretty good job. About half of my words made it on the computer. So if the whole thing had a bell curve, I would have gotten at least a B. I then printed out the paper that had alleged jokes on it.

I went into my room downstairs to take a nap. At least that's what I wanted to do. As I lied in my unmade bed, I couldn't fall asleep. I got up to try to relax, but that didn't work either. I stood there. At first I wasn't really thinking about anything or anyone. I was just there. It felt like I knew what I wanted to do, but I couldn't do it.

As I stood in my room still dazed, I thought of all the things happening in the world at the same time.

Someone is killing another person with a weapon that is never used for murder. Someone is having a baby that they don't want to have. Someone is giving a speech to a group who hates speeches. Someone is laughing at a joke that isn't funny. Someone is crying over a lost one they barely knew. Someone is getting drunk with a non- alcoholic drink. And someone is having sex with someone who they just met. There are so many more interesting things going on besides the boring story I'm telling you. I'm laughing about that as much as you are.

Have you ever wanted to not think about anything? I mean nothing. Not even prayers or meditation. Just not have to think about your awful job, lack of money, being late to class, where you put your cell phone or any other mundane worry that life throws at you. I do sometimes. When I'm really out of it, I pretend to slice a hole at the top of my head, take out my brain and scrub it, give it a nice clean. I didn't do that this time. I'm convinced that I only think because I have a brain, not because I have many thoughts worth noting.

You ever get an idea in your head and it's all you think about? Sure, you may be working or going to class or whatever it is you are doing; to an observer you're just going about your day, but that's not how it is to you. For some reason, all of your brain decided to focus on this really stupid question. As if all your brain cells teamed up and forgot about the world. You are overanalyzing some weird ass question you think you have the answer to. Because you know so much of the freaking world.

Well, that's what I did as soon as I woke up from my nap. It wasn't really a nap as much as me just passing out on my bed. Passing out is one of the oddest feelings ever. I feel like I fast forward in time when I wake up. I don't try to pass out, but I kind of don't mind it either. I was in a fog when I walked around the house. My only saving grace is that I didn't need to look for anything so I could just leave. I would have searched for twenty minutes if my wallet, keys, and joke paper weren't on the kitchen counter. There was a twenty- dollar bill I took on my way out. I don't know if it was even mine. I didn't take my car because the station is only about fifteen minutes away if I walk. I don't mind walking home after being in the city all night. There is something peaceful about going down the empty dark roads of town late at night.

As I walked down the block, I couldn't help but think about being a brain in a vat. That I had no control over any of my actions and none of them mattered anyway. For those of you who don't know what that is, then you should probably go read another book. Maybe that woman who wrote about moose decided to write a story on it. I'm going to give you a dumbed-down version of it. Kind of like one of those comedians at the open mic, and take a really complicated matter and make it really simple. The difference here is I'm talking about a philosophical theory and not a Lenny Small joke. And I won't smell of booze. Brain in a vat is a theory that states everything is an illusion. I am just being controlled by a mad scientist. So basically it's *The Matrix*, but not as cool. I don't have a body, just a brain that the mad scientist shows the world I live in. Get it? When I first heard of it, I was kind of lost, since I never heard the word "vat" used in any other aspect of my life. According to that theory, I am not technically the writer of this story, some unnamed nutjob is.

Those philosophy questions can really mess with an idiot like me, have me second-guessing, overthinking everything around me. Am I real? Are you real? Is anything real? But what is real? Is "real" just a word anyway? A word we used to describe something we may not even understand? So what if I am trying to come to a conclusion with a definition that is wrong in the first place? Oh screw it. Whatever. Fuck philosophy. It's too confusing. Whenever I think of philosophy, I seem to get more questions about the world that I can't answer.

I would have continued pondering over my own existence if someone didn't say hi to me on my way to the station.

I stumbled past a kid probably five or eight or eleven, I don't know; I'm bad at guessing kid's ages. They're all just kids to me. She was old enough to talk though if that helps. She stood outside at the side of the house of some neighbors I don't really know. Probably the only neighbors that I can't tell you a story about. She had on a blue dress so the family must have gotten back from a party or something.

She waved at me and smiled. "Hello." I never met the kid. I had no idea who she was.

I said hi back and continued down the block.

It's amazing how kids can be the nicest people sometimes. They have no agendas. They don't judge someone, because they don't even know what that means. They're too young. The bullshit in the world didn't get the best of them yet. If that was an adult outside, she may have ignored me.

I crossed the street and became a little upset knowing that the kind, good-hearted kid will be me one day; a sarcastic wiseass who has an answer for everything and thinks she knows a lot more than she really does. People will tell her how cute she was as a kid and joke about what happened to her. But I'm not sure how much of a joke that will really be. Since that kid won't be as good-looking or successful as she dreamed of.

How do you explain to kids that in the future they will look back on being a kid? Do you tell them like it's a hint in an adventure story? Do you tell them straight that they are experiencing future nostalgia and that they don't even realize it? That's one of life's funny paradoxes. You learn as you get older only to remember your youthful days when you didn't know as much. That kid has no idea that when she grows up she'll wish she could go back to her days when she was outside as a kid innocently waving to every stranger that walked by. Until she goes to a bar one night and asks herself the same question we all ask ourselves: *"What the fuck happened?"* Where did you go wrong? Maybe you should have read the posters in school differently. Maybe you should have stayed friends with that kid you grew up with. Maybe you should have been closer to God. Maybe you should have gone out with that person you met that one time. Maybe you should have listened to the fortuneteller. If you would have made one decision in your life differently, maybe things could have been different. 'Cause this is not how it should be. Your school should be calling you asking you to be a guest speaker for the students because of your great success. You should have written the Great America Novel by now. You should have been invited to *Randall's* at this point in your life. You should be in line to be the next great talk show host. But you're not. It's just you. And the current existence you call your life filled with pointless anecdotes and jokes that you tell every person that says hello. The life you wished as a kid is dead. It died as soon as you grew up and realized it was only a dream to begin with.

The weird part about this whole thing is that poor girl probably thinks I know her name.

I walked by a house on the corner that was unique in its appearance, to say the least. It's a real ugly place. The basketball hoop is still down from last year's storm, the mailbox is broken, the windows are opened; I mean, they have no glass or anything. The grass is uncut, the car in the driveway has no wheels, and there is a little fence that goes around the property that allows it to hide from the rest of the world. It's the kind of house that Huckleberry Finn grew up in. I can't even begin to speculate who lives there. I never saw anyone go in or go out. My house has an empty refrigerator. I'm not sure if this house has one. If anyone ever gets murdered in my town, this is probably the place where it will happen. I don't want to know what the owners keep downstairs.

I continued to walk down a few blocks until I got to a house of a girl I went to high school with. It didn't look as bad as the Huckleberry Finn house. Nothing does. People could live in this one. I remember that she had the body that a rock star would sing about. Way too hot for a girl in high school. At fifteen she looked twenty-five. I never really knew her. She hung out with a different crowd. From what I know, she was adopted and lived in an apartment upstairs. I saw her on an adult video recently. I won't tell you her name, but I will tell you it isn't the name I know her by.

I could go house by house with stories of my neighbors. The guy's son a few doors down from mine got accused of raping a girl. About thirty years ago, the son was in college on a lacrosse scholarship. That's when him and his buddies were put on trial for raping a girl at a party. From what I know of the case, the son got off with no charges. I can't tell you if he really did it because I don't know. I never met the man. I only know the mom and dad, who are now both suffering from Alzheimer's. The kid down the block shot himself. Not like Harry. I mean, for real. It must have been ten years ago. He was a little older than my older sister Kate. She was in middle school at the time and I was in elementary school. Dwayne and me would talk about kid cartoons on the ride to school. I didn't even know what suicide was at the time. One day the boy walked home from school, took his dad's pistol, and ended his life. Just like that. There was a girl Kasey who lived across the street most of her life; her parents have been divorced for about five years now. She graduated college about a year and a half ago and has been traveling around Europe ever since. We won't see her on this continent ever again. She's Matt's age and would play sports with us sometimes when we were kids. I don't even remember the last time I saw her. The kid on the corner is trying this luck at a career in baseball. He's too dumb to do much else. He'll probably end up as a cop. He graduated eight years ago and has been trying to get in the minors since then. He isn't good enough to make it. Not very fast, doesn't have a great arm, has no power. He'll find that he doesn't have the talent too late. Athletes always think they are better than they are. I bet athletes and actors are great friends.

I came across a tree by the road that was different than most others. I'm not telling you this because of something I learned in science class. Anyone could see it. The tree had a purple ribbon wrapped around it in commemoration of a dead kid. His name was Michael Rungee. I only learned of this because there was a picture of his name underneath the ribbon. I never met him. Wasn't much older than me though. The picture of him was one that the family took randomly as he was in the kitchen. Like his mom decided to snap a photo of him after he just got done having some rice. It's weird how the image of him after eating a meal on a casual night is the one his family used for people to remember him. He ran the car into a pole on Steed Ave. a few months back. Drunk driving. That type of thing happens a lot around here. A young person dying from a car accident or an overdose. I don't think he was the driver in the car. But I can't be sure. If you ever get into an accident, be the drunk driver, you'll live. Sober passengers never make it.

People always make dead kids out to be much greater than they were. As if we lost a young genius or the kid was going to be president, which is not the case. It never is. What would the kid have been had he not died? Just another face in the crowd. Now his face is on a tree. And the kid gets a big funeral too. Probably bigger than Mari's. Not because all the people are his friends, but because he's a kid. Dying young is handled much worse than dying old. I'm pretty sure if I died now, I'd get a big funeral, maybe even a column in the local newspaper writing how noble of a young person I was, perhaps even a dedication from Damian mentioning how determined of a reporter I was, but if I die when I'm a little older, I'll be just another person who died. Only my close friends and family would go, not people who just so happened to know me. People won't care as much at that point since my youth would be gone anyway. You're better off dying with your innocence and potential than without it. People will make you out to be a lost cause, a hero, a martyr, even if you were going to be a bum. We view the whole thing as a tragedy. No one will say this when a young person dies, though. Of course not. What I just told you is blasphemous. I'm an inconsiderate prick for having this opinion. I'm supposed to feel bad for Michael Rungee even if he was a jackass. Even if he was going to be a bum. Even if he was the cause of his own death. Tears can really clog up a person's objectivity. Sorry, but I only have so many tears in me and I'm not spending them on people I never met. I only cry for those I actually loved.

You may have noticed I said overdose as well as car accident when I spoke of death in this town. Yeah, drugs are much more common around here than anybody would like to admit. A kid from my high school class died from an overdose. His name was Akeem Ran. He was the same as Michael Rungee in that if he didn't die I wouldn't be telling you about him. A year ago he was found dead in his parents' basement. One day he is ready for college, to take on classes, be the change, the future, pick out a career that he could use to help the world. And the next day he's buried six feet under with only a newspaper article to cover his life. Between the car accidents and drugs, I'm surprised Death doesn't have his own plaque on the wall. Maybe we can even fit him in between The Jerk and that professor with the kid's book. Around here you either know someone who can get you drugs or you are the dealer. It's easy to pretend like that stuff doesn't happen. No students cheat. No teachers lie. No one sells drugs. But that's not how it really is. I wish it wasn't the case, but it is.

So what's my deal? Where are my drugs? And more importantly, can I get you some? It should come as no shock to you that I'm not very personable. I never bothered with the whole thing. I'm too much of a loner to get involved with that. I've met some people who sold drugs, but I got them out of my life before they were in it. There was a place by the tennis courts at the school where the exchange would happen. The students knew they were off school property so they couldn't get in trouble by the principal and to a passerby they were only smoking cigarettes. You have to build connections to sell drugs and that's something I'm not interested in doing. I didn't get Jacqueline's number; do you really think I'm going to get a drug dealer's number? Do I know someone who can get you some? Of course. I can point you in the right direction, but don't expect much more from me.

There are three more of these memorials on this road, each with their own decorations and flowers to make them stand out. To remind you of the life lost. I heard of each when they occurred. Normally a family member will start the conversation with a line like, "Did you hear what happened?" And then we'd both elaborate on what we know of the accident and the person. Nothing more than a few names of the victim or victims, where they lived, what they were known for or how we knew them, if we did, that is. The one from Kate's grade was the most tragic. By that I mean it had the most deaths. Five, count them, five people from her grade died in an accident a week after graduation. I'm relieved for Kate's sake and the rest of her grade that the accident wasn't a week before the graduation because the whole ceremony would be about the five kids who died. I didn't know any of them, since they were much older than me, but yeah, Michael Rungee isn't even the worst. As for the other two trees, I don't remember them that well. I can't say with certainty that I didn't know those students before they died. An accident is not new to me or anyone else around here.

I had some time so I headed to the old high school to see if anything was going on. Sometimes there's a sports game or concert event at the school. I wasn't planning on attending anything, just to make my walk a little longer so I didn't have to wait at the train platform.

In the past year the school built a new football stadium with new seats, new turf, a new entrance, the whole shebang. There's a stupid red brick walkway that people from the town could pay to have a custom engraving included on a brick. My family did not pay for this. Why did they build a new football stadium? Because that's what we need in our society, more of an emphasis on sports. We don't put enough money into it. We need more.

Seriously, the school did it so they could broadcast college lacrosse games. It had nothing to do with the students. Why don't they put any money towards other fields? Simple. Those fields don't make any money. They act like they're doing it to better the sports program or to help the students, but they aren't.

I could see that there wasn't a good chance of anything going on since the parking lot was empty. No cars means no people, which means no event.

I walked inside my former high school for the first time since I graduated. I missed Renee's graduation last year because I was sick. And yes, I really was sick. I didn't lie to get out of it. I was in bed all day.

I didn't go down any hallway in the school. I just stayed in the main lobby, where sports stars at the school would officially sign to colleges. The student, their parents, their coach, their guidance counselor, and someone at the school with a title, like the assistant principal, would take a picture for the town newspaper highlighting the sports career of the student. And when I mean highlight, I mean highlight. The athlete is never heard of again.

You think my college sucks at sports? That's nothing compare to my high school. They're lucky if one student plays in college every few years. They were so bad that guys like me were on the basketball team. We needed a roster of twelve and only eleven guys tried out for the team. Go to the gym sometime and count all the banners the school has. It won't take long.

There isn't much in the main lobby. Just a desk by the door for the security guard and a statue of an eagle since it's the mascot. No one was sitting at the desk that was made for a classroom, not security. It's like the guy went into one of the classrooms one day and took whatever empty desk no one was using. The guy probably just needed a place to sit. The lobby basically cuts the school into parts, at least according to me. Let me lay it out for you, since I know you're dying to hear about the blueprints of the school. Down one hallway was the English wing and science wing, down another was the history wing. I avoided this wing when I could. And then there was a third hallway for the gym. You never wanted to have a history class before or after an English or science class, or vise versa. If you were still in the lobby by the first bell, then you were going to be late.

I never liked high school. Probably because I wasn't much of anyone while I was there. Too dumb to be in the smart classes. Too smart to be in the dumb classes. Too lame for the cool kids. Too cool for the lame kids. I had no real talents either. I wasn't in the band or in acting club since I kind of suck at both. I told you I played basketball. I never said I was good at it. Damn, I wasn't even the best writer in my class. There were a few girls who were much better writers than I'll ever be.

One girl, Nicole, who looked emo because she was actually emo, shared her first few chapters of the book she wrote with the writing class. It was about some vampire kid who teams up with some wizard to save the world. I have no idea. I'm pretty sure at this point she has several book deals and is in a bookstore somewhere.

Between you and me, Nicole couldn't stand me. For some reason she was hailed as the best writer in our grade, though I'm not sure why. I didn't know her before the class. Maybe she won some dumb literary arts award that no one enters to give her that confidence. I guess she didn't like that a nobody like me could challenge her in that respect. She would have her friends like Sarah edit her stories before class. Then there was me, the quiet guy who doesn't have anyone check his work, write stories that are as well-received as hers. I didn't mean to challenge her, but I kind of did by accident. Must have been my great vocabulary.

Sarah, on the other hand, was a different case. Much cooler. I mean, she was one of those girls who was happy to know bands that no one else knew or dress in what no one else was wearing. Don't let her drabby clothes or chill attitude trick you, cause she was really smart too. Like she read *The Divine Comedy* as a side reading project. Apparently that book has nothing to do with comedy. All these years I thought that book was the best comedy ever. I couldn't have been more off with that one. When she was signing my yearbook she said she flat out loved me, which I thought was her being stupid. A young girl saying it but not meaning it. As time goes by, I'm starting to think that she meant it. Also she was the first person to actually like the words I put down on a piece of paper. If there's anyone who will enjoy this story, it would be Sarah.

In the middle of the lobby is the auditorium, which holds about two hundred people. There were a bunch of speakers in it during my four years. Schools like to give students speakers to teach them lessons about life. But in reality it's just a mandatory community service appearance the person needs to do. And the students view it as a way to get out of class, not as a way to learn more. I remember one guy who talked to us about drunk driving, a message we clearly missed. At one point during his presentation, which was just the guy auditioning for TV shows more than any real speech, he would do impressions. I would say that I felt like I was watching Jake on stage, but I didn't know Jake at the time. I can't tell you for certain if he was giving the speech as part of some community service, but if I found that out, I can't say that I'd be surprised. During his read-through, he bragged about how he got signatures of young people he thought would be successful. I don't think I have to tell you that he didn't ask for mine.

I try not to think too much about my high school days because I'm reminded of how much of a loser I was. And still am. High school was awful, and my college years aren't much better. As soon as I can, I'm getting out of school and I'm not looking back. I'm pretty sure if either school named the auditorium after me, I'd still be hesitant to return. I guess this is just part of my issue I told the pastor.

I saw the school janitor Dwayne pushing a garbage can towards me. He was my bus driver when I was in elementary school and is now the janitor for the high school. He may have been the janitor when I was there, but I don't think so. His outfit gave away his occupation, with his blue jeans and dark blue t-shirt that had some white lettering on it. He was one of the few drivers that was a good guy. Some bus drivers can be really strange, like they may end up on the news for murdering someone kind of weird. I bet it's all the driving around with kids all day that does it. Who do you think hates themselves more? Bus drivers or NYC mascots? Tough call. If I was either, I'd have ended up like that kid down the street. I liked Dwayne as a kid since he knew what kids my age knew: video games, cartoons, stuff like that. I know that isn't very impressive. Give me a break, I was ten. Recess was the best part of my day. He didn't recognize me as he walked by and I wasn't in the mood to bring up that I remembered him.

I was staring at the statue of the golden eagle by the auditorium doors when he approached me.

"What are you doing here?" he asked, but not in a way that someone would when they recognize someone. He spoke like he was serious.

"You mean the school?"

"Yeah. What the hell do you think I'm talking about? I told your buddy, I don't want that type of stuff around here. All the events are done for the night. No one should be in the building. Now get out, or I'll call security. Don't think I won't." He had a sternness about him that I didn't remember. Then again, the last time I saw this guy we spoke about cartoons.

"I'll leave. Sorry."

"Come on, man. You young people got nothing better to do than get messed up with that stuff." He walked past me down the hall towards the gym and kept shaking his head in disgust. "I'm tired of telling you what's gonna happen to you. Damn kids won't listen." It's always nice to catch up with people from my past.

He pushed the garbage can down the hall heading towards the gym. I exited the school to the parking lot. It was still empty. No cars. No people. Just the coolness of the night. Standing outside was an old acquaintance, Carter. We played on the basketball team, but that's as far as our friendship went. He seemed more comfortable in the parking lot than in the classroom.

"You know you shouldn't smoke. It'll you," I said.

"I'm gonna die anyway. Why do I care?"

"Well, it's bad for you."

He ignored me and continued to fill the dark night with smoke. "What're you, one of those green assholes who wants to save the penguins?" I can't believe he was right. I was sounding like that guy. I might as well have told him a fun fact about the health concerns of smoking.

"No. I don't care much for them." I think he was talking about the polar bears, not the penguins. Unless, of course, the penguins are endangered too. Which I wouldn't know about.

"You still going to school?"

"Yeah."

There was silence in the dark air. We never had much to talk about.

He let out a lungful of smoke he had been holding. "What are you majoring in?"

"Mass communications," I paused and corrected myself. "Journalism"

"Oh." Don't ever tell someone that you major in mass communications. No one knows what that is.

"So you want to report the news?"

"Not really. I always thought of myself as more of a writer, which is great since no one reads today. How is that for a fucking joke? A writer in an era that no one reads. I don't know." I felt a weird sadness come over me. "Sometimes I wish I could get away from it all. You know?" I looked at him for a response but he kept looking forward. "Everything, the people, the places, the bullshit. Just not be a part of it." I paused. "But that's not possible in today's world is it?" Once again I expected a response from him but he just stood there staring into the distance of the dark empty parking lot. Never did his blank expression change. The most he did was blow smoke from his cigarette. I continued my self- reflection. "I'm a part of the system. And that's final. There's no way out of it." He grinned for a split second. I almost missed it. "Fuck it. The world is going to hell."

"Yeah." He puffed more smoke from his cigarette. "It probably is, but just because the world is going to hell, doesn't mean you have to."

"I guess."

"You still writing?"

"Yeah."

"Good. You continue to write. Someone has to tell it like it is. Instead of all the bullshit we hear every day. Someone has to stand up to the lying bastards. Someone has to write what they feel, not what they're told. To give a voice to those with no voice at all. Bullshit can only go so far with people."

I didn't comment on that. He must have no idea that I'm not that type of writer. I can't write deep, meaningful passages with multiple meanings and elaborate prose. I just say witty jokes to move the stories along. He must have thought I was actually a real writer.

We both stood there for a few moments. I decided to make the first move and say goodbye. "I have to catch a train to the city."

"I'm not stopping you." He didn't look at me.

"I'll… uh… see you around." I knew that I was probably never going to see him again.

So did he. "Okay. When you write that great novel, just try not to make me too much of an asshole."

"I'll try my best." I started to walk away. "But you don't give me much to work with."

He chuckled as he smoked. "Fuck you. Pretentious prick."

Once I left the school, I entered what we around here call town. It's basically a block or two of stores. What kind? The stereotypical stores that you would find in a small town: the local bakery, the bank, a pizzeria, an ice cream shop, places like that. I didn't actually go past these stores since I was on the other side of the road. I walked by the local drive-through convenience store Dairy Barn on my way over to the train station. I never go in. The place is dump. My friend's mom actually thinks it's a breeding ground for terrorists. I'm serious. She thinks that since no one works there for a long time, they're biding their time there until they do their terrorist things, like blow up a building or degrade women or whatever it is terrorists do. Probably cause terror. That's the most I ever thought about the place. Ironically enough, if that place ever gets blown up, I wouldn't really care. The place is a piece of shit anyway. The sign is falling apart, there's a huge hole in the lot, and I'm haven't even gotten to the food. Given a choice between Dairy Barn and NYC vendors, I'd go with the vendors. And that's saying something.

Passed that is the barbershop, where I get my haircuts, a Greek restaurant that I never really go into, and a Dunkin' Donuts. I was never a fan of Greek food, though to be fair I never tried it. I'm so used to eating fast food and leftover Chinese that I don't see any purpose trying other foods. It should come as no surprise to you that I walked by a Dunkin' Donuts on my way to a train station. That's how they're setup. Since they know that people are most likely to drink coffee when they get on a train. Sometimes I stop and get myself something for the train ride, but I didn't this time. I can't believe how some people drink that stuff like it's water.

Waiting on the train platform is the most boring, lonely thing ever. About as much fun as my drive to school. I stand there on the empty platform that no one else is on, leaning up against the post that keeps people from falling. I would have waited in the booth that smokers go to, but I didn't want to walk all the way down the platform.

The only thing worse than actually waiting is that I have to wait as the speakers warn me to watch my step or when the train is coming. It always features some celebrity instructing me on train safety. Because a movie star or radio host knows about that kind of stuff.

After I bought my two-way ticket, I did the only thing I could do, which was wait. As I stood there, I wondered if I would help someone who was stuck on the railway as the train came. You see that kind of stuff on the news every so often. About some poor bastard that gets run over by the two thousand ton moving object. Not the most ideal way to go. If someone needed help, I'd probably point at them and say, "Hey look, that guy needs help." Then I'd look around and see that I'm the only one there. And all of a sudden that guy doesn't need help. And I'd ignore that they were going to get hit by a train. There's a philosophy question about trains I learned back in school. What was it about? Something about picking a lever, I think.

The train was on time, which I had heard ten times already up to that point, thanks to Random Celebrity #5.

I'd tell you a flashback about some memorable time I saw someone on the platform, but that never happens. Even if I did, all I would be telling you about is some random person entering or leaving the train, which I say again, is easily the most boring thing you could ever do.

Part 5 – City

For the most part, no one speaks when they're on the train. Unless you sit by a group of people who came from a concert or sports game, you're probably not going to talk to anyone while there. The most you'll say is, "Excuse me," or, "This is my stop." And if you're like me, you'll take up more than one seat.

I always get a good laugh at all the passengers with their headphones on listening to music like that kid in my philosophy class. I mean, come on, what song is so great that you have to listen to it all the time? Do you need the song to get you going and ready for the day? I guess it's like one of those inspirational posters in schools. I don't listen to music to get hyped or energized. Why? What for? If I'm tired I'm going to take a nap or go to Dunkin Donuts. I'm not pressing repeat a million times.

I'm worried about the people who always listen to music that gets them going. I don't know about you, but that kind of stuff would drive me crazy. Even if I did have an outlet for my anger, I'd still do something bad. Too much adrenaline is not good for you.

Three middle-aged guys sat in the aisle next to me. They were all dressed casual with jeans and jackets. Nothing like the guys in the city restaurant. They were discussing how one of them should get with the woman he was texting.

"I don't know man. Should I? I mean look at that?" asked the lucky man, or fool, depending on how you look at it.

The other two were also on their phones and giving him advice on his decision. I guess the guy was already married.

"I want to, but...I know—"

"Yeah, we know," one of the other guys cut him off.

I stopped listening after that. I don't have any interest in that stranger's marital problems.

There was a woman in the seats behind them reading off of her tablet, probably that great bestseller that everyone should be reading. She was focused on whatever it was, reading like it had so much info that she had to put all of her attention towards it. Elaborate prose, or confusing terminology, I don't know. I can confidently assess she was not reading this.

Behind me was a young couple in love. They had that look. You know it. The guy had his arm around the woman who was smiling as she cuddled next to her lover. Right now they love one another so much, everything is great for these two, until they either settle with the fact that they aren't going to get any better and deal with the crummy office jobs they both have, or one of them finds out that the other is cheating. Which is going to happen? I'll never know. They got off at the next stop.

As I tell you about how silence filled the train, there was one time where I had an actual conversation with someone. It must have been about a month ago, when I was going home after one of the comedy classes. A woman around my age sat next to me on the train. Her name was Michelle Jordan. The only reason I remember this is because of the famous basketball player. She was very pretty and completely out of my league. She started to talk to me when she saw I had a manila folder with the word comedy club on it. I had just come from the first day of class where Marson handed out folders for us filled with information on the class. Which was nice of them to do. I put down hundreds of dollars, they gave me a folder. Fair trade. I'm amazed that a sense of humor is always included whenever I hear what women want in a man. My thinking is because when you laugh, you're happy. Even if it's for a brief moment, you're smiling and having a good time. Women want that as much as money. Heck everybody does. Who in their right mind wouldn't? Anyway, I made a few jokes about being in a comedy class. She mentioned how she worked for her father's company and it was her job to travel to companies across America meeting various clients. Which is quite a job for someone so young. I can barely keep a job and this woman is going across the country. Everything was going fine until she told me why she was on the train. Turns out she wasn't there to see me.

"I'm getting married. This was my last business trip before the wedding."

"Oh. That's nice." My interest in the conversation went away after that. It happens when someone you think is single turns out to be engaged. I tried to keep the conversation going somehow. "When is it?"

"Next week. I'm a little nervous."

"Oh." I didn't know what to say. I was still thrown off by her even getting married.

"But that's normal." She was talking to herself as much me. "Just pre-marriage jitters. That's it." Her voice faded.

"Yeah. I'm sure it is." I didn't know what else to say. Not because I had empathy. I don't obviously. What the hell do I know about marriage, besides the fact that I don't want one anytime soon? Not much.

She got off the train before me and I never saw her again. Sometimes when I'm on the train I wonder if she went through with that marriage.

The conductor came to punch my tickets after the train left the station. They do that so no one can use the train for free. Although there have been times late at night where a passenger won't have a ticket and the conductor won't check. I put my ticket in a slot on my chair so the conductor knew I paid. I fall asleep most times when on the train so it's best for me to not interact with the conductor. I've been woken up by the conductor asking for my ticket. It's not the most pleasant experience in the world.

We must have been three stations into the ride when I passed out. I didn't wake up until we were only one station from Penn.

I had some time, about ten minutes, before the train got to Penn, so I took out the piece of paper with my jokes. I yawned the loudest I had all day as I reached into my pocket to begin editing. The drunk in the seat in front of me, who wasn't there when I got on the train, took notice of my poor attempt at writing. The guy had a brown paper bag to hide his beer from the conductor and looked as if he was about to fall out of his seat. It's safe to say he uses the same razor as Damian. His slur gave away that he was not drinking coffee.

"You…you seem like a smart guy." He paused to speak clearer. Or as clear as a drunk could speak. "An educated man. Continue to do what you're doing." He sipped more of his alcohol as he stared at the floor of the train.

"Thanks," I said, disinterested in his comment. I hate talking to drunk people. It makes me feel uncomfortable knowing that they may not remember what we were talking about. Plus some are really hard to understand when they're wasted. Drunks on the train are the only people who seem to think anything of my intelligence.

I'm never the first one to leave the train. There are always a few people who get up before the train even pulls into Penn Station. You know, because they have to save those fifteen seconds. Anyone who stands up has to hang on to the rail as the train stops. If you have never been on a train, then you should know that the trains don't stop with ease. They abruptly come to a halt.

I waited in my seat until everyone left. The old woman, the drunk, the guys on their phones, all left before me. Even the conductor and his tickets were nowhere to be found.

As soon as I got off the train I walked upstairs to the main corridor in Penn Station. I try to avoid staying on the train platform as much as possible since it smells really bad. Like someone should open up a window to let some air in, but there are no windows to be opened. The congested air is it.

Upstairs there is a platform for various entertainers to perform for money. Each time I go there is someone different. Once I saw a guitarist playing classic rock songs, another time it was a guy singing opera. None of them are as good as professional performers. Sure, they can sing better than me, but what type of accomplishment is that really? The most people will pay for them is by tipping.

This time there was an old black guy performing old school R&B music like Marvin Gaye. He, like the others, wasn't great at singing. But it was nice to hear some music instead of the commotion of all the pedestrians walking. A few people tipped him as he sang. I've seen him before as I walk in and out of the station. White suit, white shoes, white hat, white pants, the only thing black in his appearance was his skin. For such a small gig the guy really dressed up for the occasion. I could tell he does enjoy the performance. He may be the only one that does, since he sings like he's at karaoke more than a professional.

I didn't listen to him for very long because I had to go to the bathroom. Instead of using the Penn Station bathroom that's always packed, where the police officers hang around with AK-47's, I walked over to a restaurant that had a bunch of thirty to forty-year-old men and women sitting at the bar. All of them were smiling just to hold back the tears they really have from life's disappointments. None of them will ever admit it but they're looking for something. No one goes to a bar just to drink. The guys talk of their life with such reverence when they are only describing irrelevant events, like how they hit two home runs in their last softball game, or how they helped their boss solve a problem at work. As if the women or anybody cares. And the women are all dressed up with makeup trying to impress any man they see. They're not ugly, but not models either. You can tell they spent time getting prepared for the evening. The guys have on their nicest suits, which for most aren't very nice at all. The bartender is a college student using the job to pay for art school. The TVs in the background play sports games and the room has a brown tint as if someone forgot to put in a stronger light bulb. You know the scene. I wanted nothing to do with it, so I headed towards the back of the room where the bathroom was located.

The bathroom was a single room in the restaurant, which I appreciated. I didn't want to have someone take another crap next to me. As I was in there, I focused on all those jokes that I barely remembered. The funniest part of any starting stand-up is how they have to use their notes. They can't just go up on stage and let loose. They stop every few seconds and check the notes they wrote on a piece of paper and mark off each one that the audience likes. All that time spent writing material and we can't even remember our own jokes. I will say that the bathroom was clean, or as clean as a bathroom in a restaurant that is in a train station in NYC would be. The automatic dryer sucks though. I hate that my skin feels like it's about to be ripped off whenever I use it. But there were no paper towels and I was not using the toilet paper to clean my hands, so it had to do.

After I was done with my business, I headed by the main train station bathroom, which only suckers go into if they need to take a piss. There is a line for the damn thing for crying out loud. Walk a little further down the station and use a bathroom in one of the food places. Off the top of my head I can name four different places that I have eaten in that have a bathroom, yet people still go to the main one. Unbelievable. If you are ever in the city station, stop by the cinnamon roll place all the way down at the end of the strip. Walk past the pizzeria and the deli and there is a place that sells cinnamon rolls and other unhealthy crap that puts twenty pounds on you as soon as you smell them. Trust me, you have to go there. It's the best food ever. It may cause you to have a heart attack but you'll love it. Every so often I go there to get a roll or a drink that doesn't help my heartburn. It's great.

Anyway, right past the bathroom is the escalator that leads towards the street. A word of advice; if you are ever in Penn Station, stay on the right side of the escalator so that people in a rush can walk by you. It's kind of an unwritten rule. Some people don't do that and it just annoys the hell out of the walker, who is already pissed because they are in a rush to get to their office meeting, or wherever the hell they have to go. Make it easy on yourself and stay on the right side.

I walked past a corner store and a bunch of shops in the station. I went up one more escalator, and then I was officially in NYC.

When you're there, you can tell. The whole scene changes, the mood is different. How do I describe NYC for those of you who have never been? It's filled with lights. A whole bunch of lights. The city has so many lights, I'm pretty sure that they were the first thing built by the Europeans after they bought it from the Native Americans for some shells. And there were only candles back then. That's how many lights are in the city. People were talking about putting them there before they were even invented. Think about it like this; one of the most famous novels is just about a kid walking around the place. If that happens in any other city, no one gives a shit about it. But it's NYC. So people care. Only in NYC can walking around make great literature.

I heard somewhere that the city lights make it hard to distinguish what's real or not. Now I see what the person was saying. That helps me more than it does you, but whatever. That's something I can't describe. You have to just see it yourself, I guess.

You can find just about anyone in the city: good, bad, boring, fun, smart, stupid, white, black, Asian, Indian, Spanish. All worried about their own shit. That's the thing about New Yorkers; you may think they're rude because they are not talkative, because they don't stop to say hi. They're not, at least, not all of them. They just have some shit to deal with. That's all. People in the city are crude, hard, and tough. They're built to handle just about anything. I'm pretty sure when the apocalypse happens, New Yorkers are just going to look at it unnerved.

The first thing you'll notice about NYC, besides all the damn people and lights, are the street vendors. All the freaking street vendors. They sell you crap: a bootleg version of a movie you saw twenty years ago, cheap key chains, outdated devices, books no one likes. The vendors have everything. The only problem is that none of it is worth buying. Oh, and the food. Yeah, I stay away from the food vendors in the city. I don't want to die of food poisoning. That stuff makes the café food look good.

On the other side of the street was a rally against a world leader. At least I think it was for a world leader. I don't pay attention to politicians, since I don't really like liars. There were about eighty to one hundred people standing there mad at something. One guy had a megaphone and everyone would chant whatever he said. He spoke in another language, so I don't know what he was saying. I can imagine it had to do with their hatred of the world leader. I didn't stop to join the rally. Because that's what they want. A wiseass like me who doesn't speak their language to join. I saw the leader's face on four or five signs being held up. He had the jackass look of a leader. Of someone who thinks he is important. Michael Rungee did not have a picture like this. The comedians at *The Scraper* didn't either. The dictator's face was stern, as if the photographer told him to pretend to be really serious. It's the photo that will be used on the cover of the leader's memoir. The one that the people at the rally will probably burn. Most of the pictures were not just of the ugly bastard. No, that's not enough at a rally. In order to really make their frustration seen, the ralliers took the liberty to put horns on his head, with the word *"DEVIL"* under it. Maybe they went to the same store that the homeless guy goes to to buy his markers. I assume the edited version of the stoic picture is their way of saying this guy is the devil. Or maybe that's his name. I don't know. I may be making an ass of myself.

It's never good when someone is holding up a sign that states you are the devil. If that isn't a sign that people hate you, then what is? Being called Satan is probably like fifth on my list of *"Things I Never Want to Happen to Me."* Aside from being brutally murdered, tortured, raped, or brainwashed. No matter how much of a schmuck I can be, that's something I don't want. How the hell am I supposed to be funny if people think I'm the prince of darkness? Can't happen. And if I ever stood by a crowd that called me a crazy dictator, chances are I'd be running from them. Or dead.

As the city lights hit me, a homeless person sitting nearby shook his can, asking for money. I don't know his story. He could have been a veteran who got screwed by the government or maybe he lost all his money when the economy went to hell. I do know that I walked right by, not even acknowledging he needed help.

I'll admit that I felt bad ignoring the old bum. Who am I to look the other way? It hurts me that the first thought I had when I saw him was that he may be a con. Yeah. I'm sure having no arms is part of the act.

I must have been walking for about two or three blocks by then. The guilt was really getting to me. I was even tempted to go back and give the old bum some money. I didn't though. I continued walking.

NYC is the only place in the world where you can walk aimlessly and be okay. Unless you get hit by a speeding taxi, then you're screwed. As you go around NYC, a car will probably almost hit you. You're not in the city if you don't have to worry about reckless drivers running you over.

Walking around NYC is pretty repetitive. I mean, even more than reading. You go down a crowded sidewalk until you get to the corner and then you cross the street. Your expertise as a city walker will determine how long it'll take you to get over. Experienced walkers go when they see an opening, regardless of what the crossing sign reads. Inexperienced walkers, who don't know where they are going, wait for the crossing sign to turn white, which means go. As you approach your destination, you will see buildings and buildings and more buildings. At first, the view is pretty amazing, but it wears off after you've been in the city a few times

You probably think open mics are really funny. A hidden gem to find unsung, unknown comedians. Well, you're wrong. They're not. They're actually filled with a lot of sadness and pathetic losers who will never make it in comedy. Open mics are for people who need therapy but don't want to pay for it. Outcasts society doesn't care for and who have no true voice and nothing important to say. The most insight you'll get from these losers is a dumbed-down version of a Lenny Small joke. They cover up their depression with jokes and alcohol in hopes of making it in comedy, to be an actor or talk show host and leave their crappy life behind, which none of them will do.

Open mics are some of the saddest places I've been. I've attended funerals with more hope. Most comedians there are not funny. Some are barely educated. The rooms are darkly lit, basically empty, and the college café has better chairs. Fifteen to twenty wannabe comedians are all who fill the room, so if you make a joke no one laughs anyway.

You don't want to spend too much time at opens mics or you will get used to the self-deprecating hopeless culture. Open mics are not funny. Not one bit.

Most comedians are so bad at these open mics that I can barely remember them. They are just a person who spoke for five minutes of my life on a stage. Their name, their life, is so generic and boring that I can't tell you about them. At least for most of them. There are two comedians I do remember vividly and I still see every so often at one of the open mics.

I call one of the guys the Pun Guy because I don't know his actual name. Keep in mind when I go to open mics, even when I'm with Jake, I don't really pay attention to the comedians. Partly because they suck and partly because I am focused on my own jokes. If I don't write bad jokes, who will? So when that great MC called out this guy's name, I missed it. Oops.

So this guy is called the Pun Guy because, you guessed it; he uses puns while on stage. He has a big nose and tight orange t-shirt, so he's tough to miss. Although I will say I wished I never saw his comedy. Poor guy is so unfunny he actually stopped his puns one time while on stage and asked the empty room, "What? Too much with the puns?" I mean, is that ever really a question? Too much with the puns? Don't ever use puns. Ever. Unless you want to end up like the Pun Guy, asking an empty room if your awful jokes are funny. You know who is probably friends with the Pun Guy? Mr. Schmidt. Ew. The two probably tell each other stupid pun jokes all day.

"Hey, Pun Guy." Yes, even Mr. Schmidt would call him the Pun Guy. "Have you heard the one about assuming?"

"No. Please tell me."

I purposely didn't say any puns while mentioning the Pun Guy. You know why? Puns are stupid. How is that for insightful writing? You're better off cursing than using puns.

Then there's a guy who's like a million years old, who probably worked with Mr. Wenington when the school was built, who just reads from the newspaper or whatever other reading material he must have found walking around the city to create his routine. Seriously, there are no jokes in his act. All the senior does is read while he's on stage. He must have thought he was at a poetry slam. Last time I saw him on stage, he read a few chapters from *"Fuck You, I Never Liked You Anyway."* It was very bizarre to see. I just didn't get what he was doing.

There is only one other person from all the times I've been to open mics that is kind of worth mentioning. The heckler. He would sit in the back of the room completely wasted, heckling whatever comedian was on stage. He resembled the drunk on the train with his dirty appearance. He was there so much that he knew the jokes that some of the comedians were saying and he would interrupt the comedian and ruin the punchline.

I swear I hate hecklers. I'm pretty sure I'd go crazy at them if they spoke during my set. After awhile I'd bring a concealed weapon on stage and shoot down any poor bastard that heckles my show. BANG! Right in the head! Now that's a performance the audience would never forget. All hecklers should be shot. Or at least have to carry around a picture claiming that they're Satan. They don't understand the time and effort comedians put into their work. Even if it is pointless comedy like Harry's, shut up and let the man speak while on stage.

Despite this, I never had a problem with the heckler.

The name of the first comedy club I headed to is called *Broadway Comedy Club*. Since it's on Broadway, the owners of these clubs are just so clever with their names. I cut through Times Square to get there.

Times Square is like someone decided to have a block party in the middle of the city and never closed the event. You can't help but look around and think, *"So is anybody going to shut this down? Are we cool with this? Yes? We are? Oh. Okay. I'll just keep on walking."* There are stands at the end of one of the areas. Stands that would be at a football stadium, in Times Square. Why? I don't know. Why is there a big screen that everyone stops and takes pictures of? Times Square must have been the place where Alice fell down the rabbit hole, because nothing really makes sense there.

There was a cute actress giving out pamphlets for some musical about sailors, which I guess is why she was dressed like a sailor. I admit the only reason I took the pamphlet is because she was hot. I feel bad for saying that but if she was ugly, I would have ignored her.

"Go see *Sailor My Day*," she said to anyone listening.

"Are you in it?" I said.

"No. I'm just giving out the flyers for the musical." I couldn't tell if she was mocking me or if she was serious.

Either way, I took the pamphlet, probably for the same reason I went to Bible study. "Thanks."

I saw a show on Broadway with school last year. The only thing I remember about the show is that there was a woman in it who was supposed to be an ugly green witch. She wasn't though. She was hot. I was confused as to whether I should be attracted to her since they were trying to make her not human. That happens to me every so often. I will be attracted to a hot woman in a show that isn't supposed to be human. She's a witch or some other mythological creature. And this isn't just because I'm a guy objectifying women. Women have this happen to them also. Like when they are drawn to the good-looking men who are supposed to be werewolves or vampires. Nicole probably has a handsome man in her book. The idea of being attracted to something not human confuses me. Am I supposed to be attracted to that witch? Because I am.

I think there's a rule that everyone on Broadway has to be really pretty. If you're ugly they kick you out before you even get on stage. Even the ugly people on Broadway are pretty.

The mascots, well, not so much.

I forgot to mention all the damn mascots in Times Square. Elmo, Buzz, Mickey. They're all there. And you should stay away from them. That isn't really Elmo. That's a forty-year-old man who can barely speak English in an Elmo costume. The mascots must be the most depressed people in NYC, even more than the open mic comedians. How can they not be? Their job is to stand outside all day in a freaking costume. It sounds like an awful way to make a living.

As I made my way through Times Square, I saw a billboard that had a woman in a similar blue navy pinup costume to the one who handed me the pamphlet. In large blue letters it read, *"SAILOR MY DAY, WINNER OF BEST NEW MUSICAL."* Every time I go into the city there's a new musical or show being praised. I can't keep track. And if I could, I don't think I'd want to anyway.

Broadway Comedy Club has a much darker feel than the other ones. Like there's some gambling or stripping going on in other rooms when the open mics are closed. From what I know though, there's nothing actually going on here besides comedy. At least that's what they tell me.

The room is large, yet not much is in the actual room. Only one table in the back. It's probably the biggest room I've been in all day, but has the least amount of stuff in it. Normally the open mic is past the bar in the back. You get two drinks minimum because you're at the open mic. Most people abuse this policy. Culprit number one being the heckler. By the end of the night, anyone still there is drunk. And yes, I have been there all night because that's the only way to get on stage. You have to wait for them to call your name, which may take all night.

A tall guy in glasses walked by as if he was just passing through and had no intention of staying in the room. He didn't see me when I called out to him. "Hey. I'm here for the open mic."

"Sorry." He took a moment to gather himself since I was interrupting an important task like throwing out the trash or putting up a sign. "We won't have any open mics until after Halloween."

"Halloween? It's not even the end of September."

"Yeah. We'll be hosting costume parties this year." He grabbed a yellow pamphlet from the table. "Here you go. We just had one for kids finish up. Our next one for adults will be tomorrow at seven."

What the hell? Does everyone have pamphlets or flyers or paper ready to give out to anyone passing by? Is that what I need to succeed in this world? Because it seems everyone is ready to give me something every time I talk to them. Also, I'm worried that the place I told you may hold gambling and strippers had a party for children.

"Oh. That's nice." You have got to be kidding me. A Halloween party at a comedy club? I took the yellow pamphlet and headed for the exit, deliberately ignoring the helper. "Well, if I go to *The Scraper* now, I can still make it and...yeah, I'll do that," I said to myself. Sometimes my thoughts are faster than my words. What I meant was if I went to *The Scraper* right away, I may be able to make it to their open mic.

I didn't wait long to continue on my way. At every street corner is a comedian trying to sell you tickets to an event. They say it's a must watch night in comedy and try to get any sucker that walks by to attend the show.

The annoying stranger picked me out from the crowd. "My man. Black jacket." He was talking about me. "My man. Now I know you want to go to a comedy show. You need some humor in your life."

First off, I am not your man. Don't act like we're best buds. Once I walk by you I will never see you again, and I will never even think about you, well, besides this story. And secondly, I don't want to go to a comedy show. See what I mean when I say that people think I'm not funny? Even the guys selling the comedy tickets have a hard time seeing me as a comedian.

I didn't even acknowledge him and continued down the street.

A block or two after that, I saw another comedian doing the same thing. This guy wasn't as successful and didn't bother me. He was complaining at his lack of success more than approaching people. "Goddammit. Does anyone speak English? I have an easier time selling weed than this." He probably does.

That reminds me of people who ask me to tell a joke when they hear I'm trying to be a comedian. Like I have a whole routine set up just for them. What, do people think I'm a puppet and every time you pull my string I tell a joke? The way people take comedians for granted annoys me. Not as much as hecklers, but it's close. If I ever see you in the street, don't ask me to tell you a joke. I'll ignore you.

I headed down a few more blocks until outside of the comedy club I saw none other than Harry-fucking-Bent. Just the guy I wanted to see. The moron from my comedy class who writes jokes on his arms. The guy that the teacher loves for being an idiot. He could barely stand and was way too enthusiastic for my liking. I couldn't tell if he was drunk or happy or both.

"You won't believe it!" He regrouped what he could of himself. "You know the open mic that was here tonight?" He always acted like he knew more about the comedy scene than me. Like I had no clue about the open mic. As if I was just walking by for no reason.

"I'm actually here for the drinks." Because that's what I do. Go to comedy clubs for the alcohol. I love going to all the optimistic, hopeful open mics for all the cheap, limitless beverages. I enjoy hearing drunken losers tell unfunny jokes to an empty room. Harry can really be an idiot sometimes, when he is not being a complete suck up, that is.

"Randy Landfield showed up!"

I tried to make sense of what he just said. "What?"

"Randy Landfield! You know, the guy from *Randall's*!"

"I've heard of him." We all have dumbass. I'm in the same class as you. Harry must think he's the only one that pays attention.

He then reported on what I missed because he's helpful like that. "Yeah. He surprised everyone by showing up and performing for fifteen minutes. No one knew he was showing up. Not even the club! It was great. I even talked to him afterwards. He said he really likes my material. And I should contact him. I may even go on tour with other comedians he likes."

I could only think of three words to say to Harry. Three words to get my point across. Three words to shut him up. "Go fuck yourself." I rolled my eyes and walked away.

Not all of my days in the city are this bad. Two weeks ago, I had a great experience walking home from the comedy class. I'm quick to leave when the class ends. Some people like to chat afterwards. Like Dimitri. He can talk for days after class. Not me. That was never was my style. Even when I do talk to people after class, it isn't for very long.

I was walking to the train station, which is a good walk, since the station is on 42nd and the comedy club is on 23rd. Most days I carry a notebook with me, but that day I had an umbrella too because well, why do you think? I heard it would rain eventually on that day. And I was right. I wasn't even five blocks into my walk when it started to pour. And I'm talking as bad as it can get. Not just drizzles. The type of downpour that drivers have to slow down for and pedestrians avoid. I looked pretty damn smart with my umbrella. I walked a few blocks with it until I saw a large man with a cane walking slowly down the block. The guy was really getting wet. You could tell he was going as fast as he could to get out of the rain. I don't know why, but I gave the guy my umbrella when I saw him. He didn't know what to say. I think he expected me to be like most people and just walk by and ignore him. It is the city after all. Being selfish is normal here. But I hate getting wet, so I figured that guy must not like it either. And since the poor bastard had a cane he was going to get wetter in five minutes than I would in an hour. Now of course I didn't realize that I was all out of money, so I couldn't buy another umbrella. But I didn't care. I just walked in the pouring rain all the way to the station. Like I said, not all the days in the city are bad.

I made my way over to my third comedy club of the night, called *Roncho's Lounge.* I don't know why it's called that. There's nothing witty or clever in the title. It's hosted by Cherry Lovin, who is a thirty-five to forty- five-year-old woman with black hair and pretty hot for a woman her age. She doesn't hold back either, wearing low cut blouses to every open mic she hosts. All she does is tell dirty jokes in between introducing the comedians. How she had sex here. Did someone there. Dan Isles would be proud. I could never tell if she was joking or actually explaining her sex life, because she comes across as a person who had a very active sex life. Very, very active. It could have been her persona. Either way, she was very comfortable with it.

I don't go to this club much anymore because it ends earlier than the others and is always packed. It wasn't like that when I first started going. No one attended this open mic when I went with Jake. I would get up on stage and the room would be filled with only other comedians. No, not the Pun Guy or the Book Guy, or any comedians from class. These comedians were awful too. I'd tell you some of their names but I didn't pay much attention to them when they were on stage. I kept my mind on my jokes. Somewhere along the line something changed. Now the room is packed with fifty to sixty people, only half of which are comedians. My guess is that the club changed their policy for the participating comedians. They must make them bring a few guests now. It doesn't seem like much, but if you have fifteen to twenty comedians go to the open mic each bringing three people with them, it adds up quickly. I prefer to talk to an empty room.

The bar has a real old time feel to it, with posters from old movies with Deanimo and other actors who were alive before me. There is no TV or anything around the bar, only a bunch of white tables. This open mic is brighter compared to the others. It could be the glass window by the door or the yellow and brown walls.

There are two rooms in this place, one where the open mic takes place and the main room with the bar. I didn't even walk into the open mic room because I saw someone sitting at the bar. The guy had the look of someone who was up to something and wore an all black jacket with sunglasses. Normally I'd stay away from shady characters, but I really wanted to know about the open mic.

"Hey. Is there an open mic here tonight?"

The guy was preoccupied with his drink. "Nah. Sorry kid. You just missed it. It ended fifteen minutes ago."

"Oh thanks."

With no reason to stay, I left immediately.

I didn't walk very far until my anger got the best of me. "Goddammit. Fuck!" I threw an empty soda bottle I found on the ground against the nearest wall. The impact of the throw wasn't nearly as great as I imagined. In my head I thought the bottle would smash into a thousand different pieces and leave a mark on the stone wall. It didn't. It just lightly hit the wall and fell to the ground, still intact. Damn. I forgot the bottle was made of plastic.

That just got me more frustrated so I picked up the bottle and started to smash it into the blue mailbox by the curb as I cursed.

"You goddamn motherfucking cock sucking piece of shit asshole! Fuck, fuck, fuck!"

This continued for a few seconds. I'm quite good at cursing with variety when I'm mad. Each curse comes out of my mouth naturally. I don't repeat the word fuck fifty times. Cursing is the most poetic I can be. My meltdown was going fine, I was just another weirdo in the city acting oddly, nothing new, happens on Broadway all the time, until I kicked the mailbox, which was a bad move on my part, since my foot took the most damage. I cried out, "Fuck!"

At that point I gave up on my anger and I lightly tossed the bottle by the wall. I walked as fast as I could, pain and all, to Penn Station. That's not to say I wasn't still pissed off. I was. I had blinders on though. I'm pretty sure I ran over a few tourists along the way. I bumped into every person I saw without remorse or care.

One corner street was held up because of an apparent car accident. I didn't pay much attention to it. I only know it occurred because of the comments from pedestrians observing the crash.

"How sad."

"Too bad to see a thing like that."

"What a tragedy."

Typical lines people use for accidents, when they know that they should be sad, but they don't actually know the person who died. I caught a glimpse of an orange ambulance on the side of the road. I never got a look at the victim since I was too busy pushing my way through the crowd.

I stampeded through four or five blocks more after that until I realized I was going in the wrong direction. And when I noticed this, I just stopped, which is against city protocol. You never stop walking in the city. Even when crossing the streets. You just keep walking. Tourists make this mistake all the time. They wait for the crossing light to turn white to cross the streets, or they stop to take pictures of random buildings. Not even important ones. Just a random building. I never know how to tell them that the building they are photographing is not actually that significant. Amateurs. I stood for a second on the sidewalk to get my surroundings.

I was by a small park. One I would have passed by unnoticed if I had kept walking. There was a green sign with white lettering: *"WELCOME TO PAUL A. FETTER PARK."* I don't know if I'm supposed to know him or not. He may have been a politician from a million years ago. Or maybe a local person that did something. Next to that sign was another similarly looking one telling people what not to do in a park. No littering. No dogs. No whatever other crap they don't want you doing. All that good stuff. It's nice to be told what you can and can't do before you even get into the park. Very considerate.

A young woman was leaning on the fence around the park a few feet away. She had red hair, ripped jeans, and tattoos on her arms. Her shirt was barely on and she had an earing on her left nostril. You know the type. Nobody knows what she looks like without accessories on. Not even her. This woman has done everything she can to go against societal norms of fashion. You don't have to be a sociologist to see she does this in order to hide a wound she has. Maybe literally. Maybe not. She definitely has a pain that she's trying to hide from the world. I'd guess it was something similar to Natacha's, unfortunately.

At this moment, I wanted to give the poor girl a hug and tell her that it was okay. That she didn't need all the tattoos and weird hair to be happy. People will like you without all that. But I didn't. People don't like that kind of sentiment. Let me explain what I just said; back in high school I had a psychology teacher named Mr. Chapman.

You couldn't tell his ethnicity. He may have been a white guy with a great tan, a Latino guy, or a light black guy. I never really knew. He may even be related to the fat comedian Carl, who knows? He always wore a suit and had an arrogance about him that I didn't like. He thought he knew so much of the world, but he was a high school teacher. So how the hell does that work? I even got into an argument with him one day on the subject of failing. He said there's no such thing as failing. If you do your best then you don't fail. Failure is based on effort, not outcome. I said he was wrong. What the hell does that F on the paper mean then? You failed! I'm not that bad with words. Society sets standards and when you don't reach them, even if you did your best, you failed. After going back and forth for ten minutes, I stopped. Some people think their view of the world is right and there's nothing you can do about it. I still think I am right. You can't just make up reasons as to why you didn't fail to protect your ego. You lost. Get over it. Stop bitching like a YA protagonist about how you can't lose and move on. The idiot thought so much of himself that he never admitted defeat. Anyway, another day in that same class while showing a slideshow, Mr. Chapman pointed to a guy on the screen that had tattoos all over his body where it was difficult to tell if we were looking at a human. In his self-righteous way Mr. Chapman told the class, "This guy needs a hug. I just…I just want to go up to him and give him a great big hug. That's all he wants. If this man got more hugs growing up then he would not be this way."

So when I said that I wanted to give the tattoo woman a hug, that's what I meant. A hug, not for my sake, but for hers.

I said nothing to her and walked into the park to sit down for a minute. It wasn't a very big park. There was barely enough room for the one playground, where a mom and kid were sitting. The kid had red and white paint on his face.

I didn't sit on the bench next to the mom to talk. I didn't even want to check my jokes. I just needed to sit after walking around all day. And my leg was still stinging a little from that wise kick. The mom didn't have paint on her face. If she did, I would not have sat down.

"Ahhh!" the kid yelled at me once I sat down. "That's my zombie impression." It was the worst zombie impression I'd ever heard in my entire life. Someone should teach this kid how to be a zombie, if he doesn't learn so on his own.

"It's good," I said, because I'm not a complete asshole.

The mom must have taken that as a cue to talk about her son's life. "He already started the new year. Can't believe he is growing up so fast."

"Yeah." I didn't know what to say so I did my best to further the conversation. "Wait till he learns that his education is screwing him more than teaching him." Damn. Why did I say that? Sometimes I say things that I shouldn't have said. That was one of those moments.

She gave me that look that people only give to someone when they think they're a complete and utter moron. Like how did God allow such a stupid human being to even live this long? She did what she thought was the right decision and took her son by the hand. "Come on Billy. We have to get home before it's too late." She didn't want to tell the kid that the nice man they met is crazy. That was kind of her.

I didn't stay in the park for long after that. As I left, a Buddhist monk came up to me all innocently and ready for prayer. Monks never look violent. Must be all that meditating. And they always walk around as if they forgot how to speak. I'm not sure what that's about.

"Hey," I said to the stranger in a cloth. He offered me some item that I can assume is like a Catholic cross to Buddhists. And no, my book didn't cover that, so don't ask me for more about it. If a vendor down the street sold the item, I wouldn't have bought it.

I was about to take the piece when the monk reached out his other hand, as if to imply it costs something. Or that he wanted to shake my hand. I took his action to mean the former.

"Oh. No thanks," I kindly refused whatever he was selling.

Damn. Even Buddha wants my money. Get the hell out of here with that bullshit. That's why I hate religion. I don't know much about church or anything holy, but I don't ever remember Jesus asking for money. Did Buddha go around asking people for donations to help him with his enlightenment? When I die, I always imagined that God would ask me one question. Not about my jokes or my writing, but of my life. *"How many people did you help while you lived on Earth?"* I honestly don't know if I have an answer for that. And for all of our sakes, let's hope that God doesn't put my writing on his priority list.

On my way out of the park I saw two middle- aged foreign women speaking in their native tongue. Something that sounded Swedish. To me, all foreign languages sound Swedish, yet I couldn't even tell you one Swedish word. I have no idea why I think that. The two stood staring and pointing at a building, and had the enthusiasm only a foreigner could have. A person from around here would not be that ecstatic about something so mundane. No one I know is that excited about life, in general. It comes across as fake. One of them had their phone out for pictures, since they just had to capture their experience to share with others.

I didn't bother telling them they weren't looking at a landmark or historical site. It was nothing more than a random building that no one will recognize when they see the picture. But whatever. It wasn't worth confronting them about it. They may not even speak English.

As I walked back into Penn Station, I saw the same
bum that I saw earlier. This time he was on the other
side of the sidewalk.

Think about that for a second. This goddamn bastard
actually took the time to think to himself, *"What is
the better location for me to sit and beg for money? I
may be better off if I sit on the other side of the
street."* Get out of there with that bullshit. Where did
you get your marker to write your sign? Tell me that
and I will give you money. I never give money to
homeless people on the street. They are just scam
artists trying to make a buck.

That happened about a week ago. A real ugly woman
too. Looked like a witch. She probably eats children
and has a big pot in her kitchen.

The woman would con ignorant train passengers by
telling them about her sick daughter Susie. "Help me!
My daughter, she's dying and needs help. My
husband left me. I have no job and my daughter
needs an operation to live." And some people would
take the bait and give her a few bucks. Which of
course wasn't going to her daughter. Since there was
no daughter.

It must have been a Tuesday night I sat on the train to
go home and the woman did her song and dance.
Then that Thursday I saw her again, still ugly and with
the same routine. This woman didn't even wait a

week. And she kept the same story! People in the city are unbelievable.

I went down the escalator and then walked into the corner bookstore. You know, one of those stores that have everything but are never your first option to go into. They have some beer, books, bags, gum, chocolate, and a bunch of other stuff that the green people claim is ruining the planet. All of these goodies define a store like this. And of course you have never heard of the store. So you either spend a few bucks thinking you're getting a good deal, or nothing at all since you never heard of the place. The store is called *The Railroad Station Store*. In case you forgot where you were.

A stack of books and magazines were placed by the entrance so all the smart people could walk passed them. Seriously though, I had some time so I thought I would give them a look.

I opened the book on the shelf hoping to find a silly picture in the book to amuse me. I didn't find one. All I found was a page with words. I hate those types of pages. It read, *"Make sure your book has a great cover. A cover that captivates the mind of the reader and gives them the proper feel for the book."*

Uh...I don't know what that means. What the hell is a proper feel for a book? The writer of this book is probably someone who can give you a whole freaking essay on timeless element and then brag about it on his resume. As I told you earlier, I never really was one who liked to captivate people, which is probably something I should work on if I plan on having a career in comedy. I turned to a different page hoping for better advice.

"Don't curse. If you can't write a story without cursing, then you aren't really a writer."

Ah crap. I already broke that rule. It is impossible for me to go a day without cursing. I blame it on the coffee. I tried my chance with another page.

"Don't leave the back cover empty. No matter what. The first thing a reader will read is the back cover. A back cover can make or break a reader buying your book."

The back cover can make a book? Really? That dumbass description a writer puts on the back of a book to make the reader buy the book can make the book, yeah ok. Does this writer know that the back covers are made to glorify the book? Back covers are equivalent to a student's grades; it only shows the good parts of it. Ask any student to show you good grades and they will have one report card with an A on it. Besides my friends, but my friends are all idiots. Since I have pretty bad grades across the board, I may just leave the damn book blank. That's like saying a commercial can make a product. It can't. It only sells it.

That is dumb advice if I've ever read it. Has this person ever written a book? One with a plot and characters? I bet not. The guy who wrote a how-to-write-a-book can't even write a novel. If you have to read a checklist for writing a classic piece of literature then you aren't writing a classic piece of literature.

It's like one of those morons who claim, "My book will change the world!" Uh, yeah. If your book is so good, then you probably don't have to tell everyone how it will change the world. It will, you know, do that on its own. Writers, comedians, actors, it doesn't matter who says it; they all lie when promoting their work.

I put the helpful book back on the shelf and laughed. This is it. This is what I'm writing an hour a day for? For this? So that a book I slaved over is put on a shelf passed by thousands of pedestrians in the station. The book gets put right next to the latest edition of celebrity gossip news and a bag of chips. Really? This has got to be a joke. I wonder if people would even notice if this book was taken off the shelf. Probably not. The arrogance of writers amuses me. They all think they're God's gift to writing, as if what they have to say is so unique, so different. But they aren't. Most writers, like comedians, suck and are lucky to be published. I would know.

Literature has gotten too pretty for me. Every book has a really fancy cover made by an artist with a character from the book standing in a pose they would be in for the story. As if the character stopped for a photo shoot during the adventure. Then there's the back cover that explains the harrowing task of the dramatic thriller you are about to experience. Every page will have you wanting more. Of course there are three or four reviews praising the book as the greatest book ever written. You won't be able to live if you don't read this book. And what happens? You read the book and it sucks. Even literature cares more about style today than actual substance.

And what's up with book signings? Who cares if the writer signed the book or not? *Dear (insert name of reader) Thanks for reading my book. I didn't think about you when I wrote, but I want you to think I did so that you will buy more of my books.* Even writers lie to you as they sign your book. I don't ever have to worry about a book signing happening at this corner shop. It's too small. Where would people go? Actually never mind. It's the right size.

I went to a book signing once. I couldn't tell you the woman's name because I don't remember it, but the event was at the school late one night. I basically went for the same reason I went to the writing meeting (the cookies, obviously). The writer wrote a book on moose, just to give you an idea on her writing preferences. Hey, I have nothing against moose; I'm just never going to write a book about them. She had her books all laid out on a table ready to sign whatever books we wanted. Because she was just so popular, everyone wanted to read her book. Sure. Apparently she wrote other books as well, probably about polar bears, or penguins, or whatever animal will be dead by 2040. She even did a Q and A session with the small group. Writers love that stuff. As if they have so many answers to life's questions. The person writes one great line and all of a sudden they are ready to be a philosopher. They aren't though. They just like to talk about themselves. In the Q and A, I asked what I thought was a fair question. Then again, I thought my philosophy essay was good. I asked, "Is there a sort of competition you have with other writers? Do you read their works and think you should write a better story than them?"

And she laughed. The whole room laughed. As if I was joking. As if it was a line I'd use at an open mic. I wasn't joking though. I was serious. In school we are taught that your classmate could get the job over you, in comedy your fellow comedian could get the gig over you, yet when I ask a writer, a professional writer about the competitive nature of the field, she laughs as if she never even thought about it. What the hell! What type of bullshit is that? Whose ass did this woman kiss to get her book published? Clearly the woman didn't do it on her own, because if she did, she'd have an answer as to how she did it on her own.

I didn't ask another question the rest of the session because I felt too much like an idiot. I just waited 'til the end and left without ever getting a book signed. Freaking moose.

I gotta say I do love covers though. Like the ones where the author's name takes up ¾ of the cover. Since the story means nothing and probably sucks, the author uses their name (or style) to sell the book. Sometimes when I don't know the author, which is much more than I'd like to admit, it takes me a second to realize that the person's name isn't the title of the book. I'm thinking maybe it could be the main character like David Copperfield or Hamlet. It's not though. It's just the author's name. Or how about the novels that tell you they are novels? It is so thoughtful of the author to include the phrase, *"a novel by (whoever the author is)"* because I couldn't tell since I was in the novel section of the bookstore and I was looking for a novel by an author who only writes novels. Thanks for the help though.

These books where the authors are on the cover crack me up too. They always seem so damn happy they're on the cover. Like they're impressed by their own work. Get over yourself. Your book isn't that great. The plot isn't that original. And the prose isn't that well- written. When I see an author on the cover of their own book, I think to myself, *"Damn that is an ugly writer."* We writers try to look presentable, but we aren't much better than Jake and the Con Lady.

It probably looked a little weird, me laughing in the middle of the station for no apparent reason. Not many people in Penn Station crack a smile. It must be all the smoke.

I could have spent the rest of the night just looking at all the book covers and reading the back covers that interested me, flipping through more pages of "helpful" books. I've done it before. That type of stuff amuses me.

When I was done laughing, I bought a five star blue notebook at half off instead of buying a novel that I may or may not read. I figured I might have time at the station so I could work on my jokes as I wait. I have no idea why I needed a notebook with five separate dividers. It's not like I'm going to write a novel or anything. Just work on a few jokes that nobody got to hear. Oh, and now you can't say that there's nothing about this story that is five stars. There is.

As I left the store, I thought about an article I read once that listed things that writers should not include in their story. One was a young adult narrator that's sarcastic throughout the novel. The other is having the setting in New York City. Which of course helps me out in all sorts of ways. So if anyone asks, say this book takes place in space and I'm a wizard. Because apparently Miss Coxman is not the only one who hates my writing.

I walked down the stairs back to the main corridor of the station. Walking down stairs makes more sense than walking up them. I always make sure to use the escalator when I'm going up. I don't really have a preference when I go down one. That could just be me on that one.

Because I wanted time to myself so I could write a few jokes, I didn't stay by the main corridor with the big sign that tells of the train's times. Want to feel like a mindless sheep stuck in the system? Go to the main corridor in Penn Station and stand next to all the people waiting for their trains. You'll feel as worthless as anything. If you're lucky, you may even get run over by a moron in a rush to get home. I headed down a terminal to wait for my train. I'd still be able to see my train on a small screen that's in the center of the terminal. What did you think I was going to do, just guess when the train is coming in? Use that great energy I have to sense the train's arrival. I walked down a bit until it was only me in the terminal. I tossed my notebook against the wall and leaned my back against it.

I was about to give up my day, to call it a night, and I would have started writing if I didn't see her, a person I never really wanted to meet.

She saw me standing by the terminal before I could run, must have walked around looking for me. I don't pay attention enough to get away with clever dirty things like that. If I ever did cheat, I'd leave my phone out on the counter for my girl to find it or accidentally text the wrong person. Lying I can do; cheating not so much. If it wasn't for me having my head down, I would have tried to avoid her completely. Maybe report her to the cop by the bathroom. Also I was the only person in the terminal, so I wasn't hard to miss.

"Oh hey. There you are. I thought I missed you." Too bad she didn't. See what I mean about talking to people that I hate? If I wrote a story about talking to people that I like, there would be no story.

"Want to go back to my place?" She mentioned that her place was a few blocks from a stop off the subway and then spoke about a few other things, but I didn't listen. I was about done with people at that point.

Before I spoke, I already felt bad for her since I don't like this woman, and now I have to lie to her. She wasn't a bad girl either. I could tell. Just wanted someone who wanted to spend the night with her. She dressed as one of those hipster girls who loved all the new YA lit books and recited classic poetry from Poe and Frost. Ironically enough, this woman would hate my comedy. Or anything I write for that matter. I'm not a real enough writer for her. She would look at John Cage's rock and understand the message. I'd tell you more about her profile on the website but I didn't really read it.

"I… ah… I'm not really up to it." I barely kept my head up.

"What?"

"No thanks." At the time a few days ago agreeing to hook up with a stranger seemed like a good idea. Now it didn't. Men should never make decisions with their dicks. Someone is bound to get hurt from it.

She rearranged her white pocket book that was too big for a girl with her small frame. "You're an asshole." I didn't realize she knew me so well. I normally have to meet a person a few times before they come to that conclusion.

For some reason, I rationalized my opinion to decline our agreement. As if that would change her thoughts on my refusal. "But don't you want more than just sex? Doesn't that, I don't know, get in the way of it all?" I make no sense when I'm tired.

"What's wrong with you?"

"I had a long day." Plus, I didn't know how to tell her that I was broke and I couldn't afford a trip on the subway. I spent the last of my money on a notebook to write some jokes. That's what I call smart spending. I should have spent the money on a snack. I'm already regretting that decision.

She stuck her pointer finger at me. "Look, I responded to your stupid message so we could hook up. That's all. We agreed." She may have been pissed at the fact that I was the only guy who was willing to hook up with her. We weren't very pretty, unlike the people on Broadway. I already told you that I woke up looking like shit. I can only imagine what I looked like then. But we weren't ugly either. Not horror shows like the Con Lady and Jake. Those two got dealt a bad card when it came to their looks. If it wasn't for the stress of life, Molly would be very attractive. But with all the shit she has to deal with, her looks are the least of her worries. I guess we just wanted to feel the excitement that we were told was sex. To feel needed and wanted by another human being. At least one of us did.

"I'm sorry. I just think it's wrong."

"Wrong? Who are you, Jesus? People do it all the time!"

"You mean fornicate?" I was really tired. I expected her to hit me in the face at that point. She didn't though.

"Yah." She tried to contain her anger. "Don't ever message me again."

As she walked down the terminal, I could hear her saying mean things about me. "He's a prick. He's a moron. He's a bad storyteller. Fuck him." All stuff I have heard before. Still, I'd much rather be the one insulting people than being insulted. I continued to stand there staring at her until she turned down the main corridor.

I thought as she left that maybe I am an insecure prick who can't see an easy opportunity when presented to me. But for some odd reason, I felt it was wrong, wanting her just for sex.

As I picked up my notebook and sat down on the ground, I couldn't help thinking that there has to be something greater than all of this. Greater than death, or hope and promise, disease and destruction. Something that sex can't relieve and money can't buy. Religion can't answer and science can't solve. There has to be something greater than all of this. There has to be. Right?

Or maybe I'm just upset over the fact that I couldn't get laid. Or maybe I'm just that exhausted. I don't know. My mind wanders when I'm tired.

That's it. That's all I have for you. What? What else do you want from me? There's no more plot or flashbacks or anything else for me to really bring up at this point. I have nothing else to write.

I'm pretty sure that this is the part where I leave you with a philosophical comment that you, the reader, can relate to because of the empathy you have towards my character. We have basically bonded through these pages, even though we really haven't. Or whatever. It must be because of how great of a storyteller I am. So descriptive. You'll think to yourself that I see the world in such a unique way and feel like I'm talking to you and you'll read into my simple remark more than I ever imagined. Because really I just wanted to end the damn thing, not get a degree in philosophy, but you don't know that. You thought I was talking about life or some deep purpose. This ending should be something like that. Whatever.

So go ahead and misinterpret this book. Ban this book because of its content (damn curses). Burn this book. Teach this book. Use this book to affect your life. Have a character in a movie carry this book around. Kill someone because of this book (don't). Become inspired to change the world because of what I told you. Pick this book for that book club you just joined. Recommend it to a friend. Read the spark notes version and learn that the one character at school was just a metaphor. Learn what a book critic thinks of the words I wrote here. Give this literature masterpiece five stars and praise it. Or give this stupid story one star and criticize it. Put this book on the best books ever list. Put this on the worst books ever list. Love this book. Hate this book. I don't care. All I know is that I will have to finish this because every story ends eventually anyway. Even this action- packed thriller. My bad if this story bored you. I told you I wasn't much of a writer. I knew I should have been more crazy. There isn't enough angst here. Next time I'll kill someone before I write a story to add to the drama.

And with that being said, my story officially ends.

Along with myself in a way. Since my life as a journalist is already dead, my life as a comedian never got going, and my life as a student won't be much longer. I don't imagine I'll ever write this much ever again. So these are probably the only words you'll ever read from me. Unless I become like one of those names in literature that publishers sell notes that I wrote on napkins just to make a buck. My "character" will have a sequel, or a spinoff, or even fan fiction to feed the demand for more of my "stories." Which I say is bullshit. This is the only story I've written. Don't let people who aren't me tell you otherwise. All you wiseasses out there who are clapping sarcastically to my departure, you got me there. But then again, if you hated what I wrote so far, why are you still reading this? Just to see how it ends? Sucker. And if you want more words from me, which I don't know why you would, well...then...may I suggest rereading this book? Since it has such a timeless element. And if that doesn't do it for you, tough luck. You enjoyed a book by a guy who most likely won't write another book. Look at the bright side; I didn't drag this crap out into twenty books just for profit. So there is that.

I could end this with a funny comedic twist. You know, to show you how funny I am. I don't want to spoil anything, but I'm kind of dead and this is all a dream. Oh no! I ruined the twist that isn't even really a twist! I shouldn't have made that joke there. I know someone is going to read that literally and think I'm actually dead and that this is a dream. The verdict is still out on whether I'm even funny.

Before I ramble on anymore, because I haven't done that enough, I'll stop writing these words for you to read. It's probably best if I just end the story here.

Acknowledgements

Thanks to my family for supporting me through the writing of this book.

About the Author

Greg Luti is an author and poet. He has written a poetry book, Collected Poems, and a short story collection, Everything Must Go. You can learn more about his books at his website, gregluti.com

www.ingramcontent.com/pod-product-compliance
Lightning Source LLC
Chambersburg PA
CBHW070344200726

48294CB00003B/782